I0745720

Books by Michael Lister

(John Jordan Novels)
Power in the Blood
Blood of the Lamb
Flesh and Blood
The Body and the Blood
Blood Sacrifice
Rivers to Blood
Innocent Blood
Blood Money
Blood Moon
Blood Cries
Blood Oath

Cataclysmos Series
Cataclysmos Book 1
Cataclysmos Book 2

(Remington James Novels)
Double Exposure
Separation Anxiety

(Merrick McKnight Novels)
Thunder Beach
A Certain Retribution

(Jimmy "Soldier" Riley Novels)
The Big Goodbye
The Big Beyond
The Big Hello
The Big Bout
The Big Blast

(Sam Michaels and Daniel Davis Series)
Burnt Offerings
Separation Anxiety

(Short Story Collections)
North Florida Noir
Florida Heat Wave
Delta Blues
Another Quiet Night in Desparation

CATACLYSMOS

a post-apocalyptic thriller

Book 1

by Michael Lister

Pulpwood Press
Panama City, FL

Inquiries should be addressed to:
Pulpwood Press
P.O. Box 35038
Panama City, FL 32412

Lister, Michael.
Cataclysmos / Michael
Lister.
-----1st ed.
p. cm.

ISBN: 978-1-888146-66-4   Hardcover
ISBN: 978-1-888146-65-3   Paperback

Book Design by Adam Ake

Printed in the United States

1 3 5 7 9 10 8 6 4 2

First Edition

For Aimeé

With affection and appreciation
of our wonderful childhood.

Thank You
Dawn, Aaron, Jill

Part 1
This is the Way the World Ends

1

The end.

This is the way the world ends
This is the way the world ends
This is the way the world ends
Not with a bang but a whimper.

Eliot had been wrong.

When the inevitable end finally arrives, it comes with neither a single bang nor whimper, but a series of sighs and death rattles, concussive bangs and barely audible whimpers, fires and floods, complete collapses of both the billion-years-work of the natural world and the thousand-years-work of civilization.

When the end comes it comes with astonishing speed.

It has been a slow build to the brink, but once the point of no return has been breached, night falls fast.

Bangs and whimpers. Different disasters, avoidable and not, and the inhuman responses to humanity's existential crises, every tipping point tipping us over the ragged rim, into a black abyss from which there is no return.

No one knows much. There is only conjecture, speculation, deduction. Most survivors only know the particular devastation they have been spared from. He has yet to hear a unifying theory for the underlying cause. And no one he has yet encountered knew any more than he did about anything but their own particular end of the world.

It makes a certain sense to him.

The birth of the universe had always been shrouded in a singular impenetrable mystery. Why shouldn't its death be?

Of course, it's nothing nearly as grand as all that. It's not the end of the universe, just of earth—and maybe not even that. More likely it's just the end of mankind—at least in any kind of meaningful way.

The end.

Of course, the end isn't only an end, but a beginning, a bleak, brutal beginning.

Dawn of a darkness devoid of grace and beauty.

Birth of a stillborn world.

2

Barren wastelands border entire towns submerged beneath black bodies of water. Empty cities, the dead their only inhabitants, surrounded by sections of scorched earth where fires still burn, embers still smolder, and ash still falls like smoky snow from a charcoal sky.

Gray days.

Every element a pale, muted pewter.

Slate sky above. Ashen earth below.

Weak currents of wind carrying ashes like bits of dried snowflakes across the lifeless landscape.

3

Twilight.

State Road 73.

Two-lane rural route connecting US 231 and Highway 90 in North Florida near Marianna.

Figures in the dim distance.

Walking this way.

Gray shadows stretched across a gray landscape.

One tall and hunched, stiff and awkward, slower. The other shorter, darker, nimble, walking warily.

He steps deeper into the woods, into the pines and live oaks, the resurrection fern and wild columbine lining the rural highway, and watches.

It's his custom not to walk on but beside roads. From a few feet within whatever foliage lines the particular thoroughfare he's following, he can keep an eye on the street without being detected himself. It makes for far more difficult terrain to travel, but what it costs in pace and pain it pays in safety and security.

He's in a hurry to get where he's going, but is convinced the slower, more arduous route is the faster route, the only route that gives him any chance at all.

Stepping a few steps deeper into the forest, the dry, brown resurrection fern crackling beneath his feet, he waits and watches.

He scratches at the too thick beard beneath his bandana and attempts to roll the tightness and tension out of his neck and shoulders.

The rural road is empty save the two figures, random debris, and the occasional abandoned vehicle. Grass and weeds have already begun to stretch through its cracks and crevices. Soon it will be completely overgrown, buried beneath an angry natural world attempting to blot out all signs of the civilization that tried to destroy it.

As they grow closer, he can see that it's an old white man and a young black guy. They appear unarmed, innocuous, but he's thought that about other survivors before. Wrongly. And it cost him.

Can't be too careful.

He crouches and watches, letting them pass.

The old man is tall and thin and wears an old once white now charcoal cowboy hat.

The old man looks harmless enough, but there is menace in the young man, and unlike so many of those who remain, including himself, he is not only not emaciated, he has retained much of his muscle tone.

How empty the earth is now, he has no way of knowing, but he encounters fewer and fewer living souls as he continues his journey south toward those he will forever feel responsible for.

Everyone he encounters—or avoids encountering by careful concealment in kudzu and the understory growth of pine tree forests and hardwood hammocks and ash piles and even among the dead—is heading in the opposite direction from him.

Rumors and reports all say the same thing. It's worse along the coasts. Of the myriad massive existential events that have befallen the earth, at least one billowed in from beyond the wall of blackness out in the raging seas. The Gulf of Mexico is no exception. In a great ironic reversal, people en masse are evacuating instead of exodusing into his home state of Florida.

When the two men have gone, he continues.

Up ahead, some fifty feet in front of him and down in the road, an overturned FedEx truck partially blocks one lane of the highway.

He wonders if it's worth a look, a quick search of the back to scavenge the packages for supplies.

He assumes it has been done a hundred times already, but the doors of the vehicle are shut tight, like eyelids against seeing the way the world is now.

He has only taken a few steps when . . .

—Hey neighbor, the old man says behind him, his voice friendly, alarmingly disarming.

He turns, his hand on the weapon in one of the duffel bags swinging from the straps across his shoulders.

Had they seen him? Smelled him? Heard him? Had he been careless? How?

—Yes, you in the woods. Hey there.

The two are standing in the empty road looking in his direction. No visible weapons. No obvious threat but the young man himself.

He slowly pulls down the damp bandana covering his nose and mouth.

The bandana is white with a black paisley pattern, which matches his urban camo pants and head wrap, black t-shirt and boots. They were the only things left in the Army Navy and Outdoor stores he had looted, but were in a way perfect for the burned-out and ashen world he was presently making his way through.

—Hey, he says, his voice not unfriendly exactly, but guarded.

—You're headed the wrong way, brother, the old man says.

He shakes his head.

The two men begin moving toward him.

Tattered clothes. Worn shoes. Oily skin and hair. Ashen faces. Everything dusted with a patina of white powder.

He eases out of the woods, down into the ditch and back in their direction to meet them near a child's over-turned red wagon in the middle of the highway.

—You military? the young guy asks.

He shakes his head.

—Police?

He shakes his head again.

He'd just robbed a store that those types frequent, but he isn't going to tell the young man that.

—I can see you're suspicious of us, the old man says. We mean you no harm. We're the good guys. Are you?

—I am.

—Not many of us left. Keep gettin' picked off. No world for the good. It's a pleasure to meet a fellow pilgrim, the old man says, extending his hand.

He eases his hand off the weapon in his bag and brings it out to shake.

The old man must be in his seventies, but his weath-ered face contains a youthful countenance and his blue eyes have a distinct sparkle.

—I'm Augustus Milton McAndrews, Sr., the old man says. Most people call me Gus but I prefer Augustus. My quiet companion here is Chandler Jackson. Goes by CJ.

The old man's mouth is dry, his parched throat tight from thirst.

The two men may not be as emaciated as the others he's encountered, but they are dehydrated.

—Nice to make your acquaintance, Augustus, CJ.

He extends his hand to shake CJ's, but receives only a knuckle bump from the early twenties-looking young man.

—Don't want to give us your name, partner? Augus-tus says.

—Doesn't seem to matter much anymore. Name's

Michael. He then smiles and adds, Most people call me Mike, but I prefer Michael.

—Well, Michael, where you been? Whatcha seen? What can you tell us about the new world?

—Was in Atlanta when it got bad. Got injured. Took me a while to get out. Been making my way back to Florida ever since. What I've seen is death, destruction, a new Dark Ages. Not much else.

He had survived the riots of Atlanta, but it had taken time for him to heal from his injuries. He had eventually gotten out of the city, but the cost had been enormous. What he had done, what he had been willing to do. Who he had become, who he's still willing to become. To survive. To save his family. To be with them again. Will they recognize him? Will there be anything left of who he used to be, of who they used to know?

—I come up out of Florida, Augustus says. Little town called Cottondale. Met this young man near Marianna not too long ago. Been traveling together today.

—That's where I'm headed.

—Need to change your course, friend, Augustus says. Further south you go, the worse it gets. A lot worse. And that's the parts that aren't underwater. Why you think we're headed north?

—Can't.

—How bad's Atlanta? CJ asks.

—Bad.

—How bad?

The city was war torn, dead littered, decimated. Those remaining dividing along the usual lines, fighting for resources.

—Real bad, he says. Avoid it if you can.

—Can't.

—I understand that.

—Whatever's there can't compare to what's waiting in the direction you're headed, Augustus says. All manner of malevolence floats in from the ocean—in the water and on the air. Comes ashore. Kills. And worse.

—Can't be helped. Have to go.

—It's suicide.

—My family's there, he says.

—Not anymore.

—Have to see for myself.

—Even if it means dying to do it? Augustus says.

—No desire to live without them, he says. Not in any world, but especially not in this one.

Scattered.

Unusual for them, when the end came and the beginning was born, they were not in relative proximity to one another, but dispersed about like random, unrelated countrymen during an unintended diaspora.

Flung far from his North Florida home, he had been in Atlanta when the end began. His wife, Dawn, unaware of his whereabouts because of an ill-conceived surprise he had been working on for her, had been at work in their small-town home of Wewahitchka.

Wewahitchka is a tiny town between Panama City and Tallahassee along the Apalachicola River and the Dead Lakes, about twenty-five miles from the Gulf of Mexico.

The town reminds him of his wife, for the two are forever linked in his mind. Dawn is a beautiful country girl, strong and resilient and capable, and he has little doubt that if she was not killed by the initial cataclysms, she will have found a way to survive.

His grown daughter, Meleah, had been in Marianna for training, his grown son, Micah, in Panama City for school. His youngest son, Travis, in Port St. Joe with his mother. His wife's son had been at Fort Benning in Columbus, Georgia.

He assumes his retired parents had been at or near their home in Wewa, but he has no idea.

He intends to find them and as many of his friends as he can and do what he can for them.

He's not heroic. But he's here. And he's got to do something. He'll start with family and close friends and move out from there. He'll do all he can for as long as he can, no matter how little and how limited that may be.

When the balloon went up, he was some three hundred miles from those who meant the most to him—miles that before the end would have taken hours to travel and were now taking more than a month. Which with the month he was detained before even beginning the journey means he is beyond late for the mask of the red death ball, every passing moment greatly decreasing the odds of finding any of his friends and family alive.

Miles. Months. Odds. None of it matters. He'll travel any distance, across the span of any time, to find them, to get them to safety if such a thing still exists, to see if he might have with them some semblance of a life, if such a thing is still possible. In the absence of any of this, of safety or even life, he will find out their fate. He will hold them in his arms if they are among the few remaining with something like life left in them. He will bury and mourn for them if not. Unless, of course, he loses the little life left inside him before he is able to close the miles and months between them—an outcome that seems more likely if not actually inevitable every moment of his post-end existence.

—How bad is Dothan? the old man asks.

—Nothing like Atlanta, but it's bad. Yet to find a place that's not.

—Dangerous? the old man asks.

He nods.

—What's more dangerous, the old man asks, the cities or the roads leading to them?

—Both are deadly, he said. Just in different ways.

—Never seen nothin' as bad as Marianna, the old man says. And only got a glimpse.

—Got any food in those bags? CJ asks. Or clean water?

He hesitates.

In addition to all that he has stuffed into the pockets of his pants and shirts and jacket, he has a backpack strapped to his back and a duffel bag dangling from each shoulder—all filled with the supplies and equipment he estimates he needs to complete his mission, which, of course, includes food and water.

—A little, he says, finally. Not enough to kill or die for.

—We ain't like that, CJ says.

—Then you are truly unique among the men I've encountered out here.

—Did *you* kill for it? Augustus asks.

—I didn't, but don't think I won't.

—You look like a pack mule, Augustus says.

—Homeless man more like, CJ says.

—We're all homeless now, he says.

—You be willing to share a few drops of water and a few morsels of food? Augustus asks.

He thinks about it for a moment, then nods his head.

He actually keeps a small portion separate to share.

—Y'all have a seat and put your hands palms down on the asphalt. Keep 'em where I can see 'em.

—That ain't necessary, CJ says.

—Yes it is. And it's nonnegotiable.

—I ain't doin' it.

—Suit yourself.

—I'll do it, Augustus says.

—Has to be both of you. And it has to be now. Got no more time to waste on this.

—Come on, CJ, Augustus says. We can't afford to be—

Screams.

Shrieks.

Struggle.

All three men spin around in search of the source.

The moment after he realizes it's coming from the back of the overturned FedEx truck, its bottom door bursts open and a small, naked young girl wearing a dog collar around her neck runs out.

The collar is connected to a chain, which trails loudly behind her as it scrapes across the asphalt.

The grimy girl is pale and gaunt with biggish breasts for her size and a dark patch of pubic hair roughly the same color as the matted mess atop her head.

He guesses she's seventeen or so, but it's hard to tell in her current condition.

She's screaming and flailing as she runs toward them.

—HELP ME. PLEASE. HELP ME.

CJ is already moving toward her.

Suddenly the chain is jerked taut and she is yanked back, her feet coming out from underneath her as she crashes onto the pavement.

A fat, redheaded, hairy man in an open kimono appears at the back of the truck, the other end of the chain in his gloved right hand.

Beneath his enormous hairy belly, his flaccid phallus is barely visible in the wiry thatch of red pubic hair.

—Where d' you think you're goin', little kitten, he says. Ain't done with you yet. Not by a far sight.

Writhing on the ground, one hand on the collar, one on the chain, the girl is still trying to get away.

That's when Michael can see the trickles of blood on her bottom and inner thighs.

When CJ reaches her, he kneels down to help her up, but the feral creature kicks and hisses at him.

—Thought you wanted help, he says. *I'm* help.

—Away from her, nigger, the fat red-headed man says. She's mine.

—The fuck d' you call me? CJ says, standing. You fat, little-dick motherfucker.

The fat man brings up a .45 semiautomatic with his non-gloved hand and begins firing, the first rounds ricocheting on the pavement.

The girl screams.

CJ dances around attempting to avoid the bullets, reaching into his coat and coming out with a pocket knife as he does.

Augustus ducks and runs for the ditch.

Michael brings the 9mm out of his bag, lowers both

duffels to the ground, then starts toward the man.

If he fires from back here, he'll be no more accurate than the fat man.

Making a wide swing, he runs up the right-hand shoulder of the road, clicking off the safety and sliding a round in the chamber.

One of the fat man's rounds clips CJ in the leg and he goes down.

Now with CJ and the girl on the ground, the fat man begins firing down in their direction, grouping his shots, greatly increasing the odds of—

CJ takes a round in the shoulder, then the neck, then the chest.

The traumatized girl gets even louder.

Screaming for help, cursing the fat man, something else he can't make out.

Then a round hits the pavement beside her and ricochets into her head.

Full stop. Instantly. No sound. No movement. A short, unhappy life over.

The fat man now turns his attention to Michael moving up toward him and begins to fire.

Stopping abruptly, Michael kneels on one knee as if about to propose, extends his arms, sights his large target, takes a quick breath as bullets buzz around him, then begins squeezing off rounds.

Aiming at the center of the fat man's enormous mass, he quickly finds his mark.

Three quick rounds in the fat man's midsection, but he neither goes down nor stops shooting.

Bullets still buzzing about him like angry bees, Michael raises his weapon and aims for the fat man's fat head, and squeezes off two quick rounds.

Both miss.

But the fat man's enormous red head explodes anyway in a crimson spray of blood and brain matter that splatters onto the white body of the truck.

Michael turns to see Augustus holding one of the

rifles from his duffel bag in the middle of the road.

He hesitates a moment, waiting to see if the old man intends to turn the weapon on him, but stands when Augustus drops it on top of the open duffel.

Silence.

As the last of the echoing gunfire fades and dies, the forest surrounding them grows as still and silent as death.

—Nice shot, Michael says as he reaches Augustus.

Augustus doesn't respond and doesn't seem to want to talk about it.

—Can't imagine the hell that poor girl has been living in, Michael says. Glad it's over. Wish we could've saved her.

—You and CJ did all you could. That's all you can do. Now all we can do is bury them and—

Michael shakes his head.

—Can't bury them, he says. Wouldn't bury the fat bastard anyway, but can't do any of them. Take too much time and energy. No way someone didn't hear all the gunfire and is on their way to check it out. It'll be dark soon. We've got to move. Now.

—All that poor girl's been through and you gonna leave her little naked body out here on the road for any and everyone to see and buzzards to pick her bones clean? Not to mention the young man who tried to save her.

—No, I'm going to drag their bodies into the truck and close it up. It's all I can do for them. Wish I could do more, but it's not something this world allows.

Before Augustus can respond, a medium-sized cur bounds out of the back of the truck. Lab and Catahoula mix, he has a blue-silver coat with a plethora of big black spots and bright blue eyes that radiate intelligence.

It's one of a very few animals he's seen since the end.

Dragging a leash behind him, he runs directly to the girl. Nuzzling. Sniffing. Licking. Then mourning.

It's obvious the dog has been better cared for than the other poor creature also in collar and leash.

—Well, hey there sweet boy, Augustus says. Aren't you a handsome fella.

The end of his leash is frayed and covered in slobber—something the animal has most likely just done in order to get to the girl.

—Guess we better check the back of the truck before we do anything else, Michael says.

They do.

Finding no other living beings, they take what little useful items they can easily find, place CJ and the girl inside, and close the doors.

—Mind if I say a few quick words? Augustus asks.

—Not at all.

Augustus removes his hat and holds it over his heart.

—Father accept these poor souls into thy keeping . . . Let them hurt and hunger no more. Amen.

—Amen.

Michael then hands Augustus some water and food, the two men shake hands, and they part company heading in opposite directions, the old man holding the leash of his new travel companion. There is neither time nor call for anything else.

4

Nocturnal noises.

Inhuman.

Insufferable.

Full dark beneath a starless sky. Zero light. Absolute black.

He travels mostly at night.

During the day he naps and scavenges and, when any sunlight at all penetrates the caustic ash and cloud coverage, charges his solar battery packs.

All his movements during the day are along the edge of the woods, but at night he runs the road.

Light in one hand. Weapon in the other.

He's developed a certain rhythm, an approach to maximize progress and minimize detection.

Light on. Beam bouncing across road and shoulder and fringe of forest, the tiniest of beacons in a sea of tyrannical and brutal blackness.

After sweeping the entire area around him from differing heights and a variety of angles, he moves from one side of the road to the other, then sprints some fifty feet and repeats the process from a different location.

Nothing can be seen in the darkness. Absolutely nothing.

Night is now about what can be heard.

He is most vulnerable when scanning his surroundings with the beam, so he limits the light and moves constantly.

Once the light is off and he's running headlong into the darkness on a trajectory other than the one the placement of his lamp would have predicted, there is only the chance—or is it eventual certitude?—of collision.

Racing down the road.

Night-blind.

Winded.

A single earbud dangling down around his chest, the other in his left ear playing a literary mashup he made while recuperating in Atlanta.

Literature had saved him—before and after the end. Since this long, dark night had befallen the earth and its inhabitants. During his many long dark nights of the soul before any of this ever began.

His bags are heavier than they have to be because of the books they contain, and he burns most of the little solar power the wan sun provides on the little listening devices that put the words in his ear and mind and soul.

King Lear and the King James Bible. Poets Rumi and Hafiz. Literary audio juxtaposition.

This cold night will turn us all to fools and madmen.

The weight of this sad time we must obey,

Speak what we feel, not what we ought to say.

And I saw in the right hand of him that sat on the throne a book written within and on the backside, sealed with seven seals.

And I saw a strong angel proclaiming with a loud voice, Who is worthy to open the book, and to loose the seals thereof?

Nothing can come of nothing.

He wills himself to focus on the ancient words

being whispered in his ear. Not the night. Not the grisly, gut-wrenching noises coming from the wicked woods. Not the darkness darker than night and the horrors it conceals.

But it's no good. He can't concentrate for more than a line or two at a time before his attention is ripped away by the appalling din in the short distance.

Blow, winds, and crack your cheeks! Rage! Blow!
You cataracts and hurricanoes, spout
Till you have drenched our steeples, drowned the cocks!
You sulphurous and thought-executing fires.

Listening to *King Lear* makes him think of the sad old man's children whose thanklessness was sharper than a serpent's tooth.

His thoughts quickly turn to his own kids who were opposite in nearly every way from the crazy old king's kids and were among the best people he had ever known, the best friends he had ever had. His broken heart aches for them, longs to know they are okay. But how can they be? How can anybody be?

And no man in heaven, nor in earth, neither under the earth, was able to open the book, neither to look thereon.

And I wept much, because no man was found worthy to open and to read the book, neither to look thereon.

Specters appear in the dark. Images he'd worked hard to suppress.

Death. Dismemberment. Decay.

Unimaginable horrors. Unforgettable nightmares.

In his previous life he had been a novelist, and he remembers writing about a character who suffered from PTSD.

I am that character now. I have become what I had before only barely imagined.

Snap. Light on. Moving. Scanning the area. Blurry vision. Unfocused eyes, unable to adjust. Sweeping all directions with the bright beam. Moving.

Random overturned vending machine in the road.

Snap. Light off. Moving. Changing sides of the road. Making a hard target.

Running.

Fear.

Focus.

And there went out another horse that was red: and power was given to him that sat thereon to take peace from the earth, and that they should kill one another: and there was given unto him a great sword.

And I looked, and behold a pale horse: and his name that sat on him was Death, and Hell followed with him. And power was given unto them over the fourth part of the earth, to kill with sword, and with hunger, and with death, and with the beasts of the earth.

Unable to take another second, another syllable of King James or *King Lear*, he presses a small button on the device in his bag and Rumi, his favorite poet, turns his thoughts to Dawn.

When I am with you, we stay up all night.
When you're not here, I can't go to sleep.
Praise God for those two insomnias!
And the difference between them.

As he races through the darkness alone, completely, utterly alone, he thinks about all the nights they had spent in the sweetest, most intimate insomnias, and how he'd give anything to be with her again. She is his home and he hers—and they had been even before they met, long before either of them knew it.

The minute I heard my first love story,
I started looking for you, not knowing
how blind that was.
Lovers don't finally meet somewhere.
They're in each other all along.

Though the line from Hafiz isn't played, he hears it nonetheless. It echoes through the empty chambers of his heart.

Ever since happiness heard your name, it has been running through the streets trying to find you.

She is his happiness and he is running through the street to find her.

Stop. *Snap.* Light. Something in the road. Move.

Abandoned ambulance. Broken windshield. Rotting body partially hanging on hood.

Scanning the area.

Moving.

Snap. Light off. Walking now. Unable or unwilling to run? Comes to the same in the end. Everything does.

Utterly exhausted.

He is a youthful mid-forties man who had played basketball and worked out throughout his entire adult life. He had even foolishly thought of himself as fit. He had not been. He still isn't—even with the fifteen or twenty pounds he has lost so far, even with the nightly running he has been doing. He is no match for this world and he knows it.

Find a place and rest.

No. Must keep going. Lost too much time already. Getting close now. Have to keep moving.

Can't.

Have to.

Are any of them even there? Any of them still alive?

Have to find out for sure.

When he's gone as far as he possibly can, he begins to search for a place to rest. Eventually, he finds an SUV in a ditch.

Carefully checking every inch of the vehicle and the area surrounding it, he drops his duffels and removes his backpack. Shoving them beneath the vehicle, he slides in behind them. Backpack beneath his head, duffel on either side, their straps looped around his arms, he withdraws one of his weapons and sets it on his chest, safety on, finger still on the trigger guard.

Then sleep.

Then dreams.

Finding his family dead. And not just dead. Decaying. The young man he killed in Atlanta telling him that's what he gets for killing him. Encouraging him to kill himself.

He wakes to a beast eating his face.

5

The dog from yesterday, the black-spotted cur, is there with him beneath the vehicle, licking his face, barking at him to wake up.

—Hey neighbor.

—Augustus?

Augustus is there too, down on all fours beside the SUV, peering in after him.

—It's me. Don't shoot.

—What're you doin' here? he asks.

—Looking for you.

—For what?

—If you wouldn't mind, Jackson and I would like to join you on your journey.

—*Jackson?*

—Our new dog.

—*Our?*

—Uh huh.

—Think you could call Jackson so I can climb out?

He does.

Michael tucks his gun into his jeans, gathers his bags, and eases out.

As soon as he's out and his eyes adjust, he surveys the gray morning and the area surrounding them.

They're next to a farm. Fences down. Empty pastures. Dead Bahia grass brittle in the breeze.

—You wanna go with me? Michael asks.

—We do.

—Why? You're the one who said I was going in the wrong direction.

—You are. But sometimes the wrong direction is the right one. I don't have long. Figure it'll be a little longer if I'm with you. Have no desire to strike out on my own—even if it's in a better direction. Jackson needs a good home and I think we can give it to him. And who knows, if you do have some family left alive, maybe I can help you find them.

Michael doesn't say anything.

—I won't slow you down much, Augustus adds. And I'll make up for it by keeping watch and offering two old helping hands when needed.

—I'm sorry about CJ, Michael says.

Augustus nods.

The dog, who has been moving about the two men, circles a time or two and flops down on the ashen ground next to their feet.

—Why Jackson?

—Found him in Jackson County and it makes him a namesake of both CJ and Andrew Jackson, Florida's first military governor.

—Whatta you think is in the woods? Augustus asks. You ever heard such horrible sounds?

Michael shrugs, but maintains the same pace, sensing Augustus wanting to slow down even more.

—I've heard things, Augustus says. Rumors.

—Been a lot of those from the very beginning. Mostly misinformation.

—But those noises, those . . . They're real. *They're* not a rumor.

Michael nods.

—You think they're human or . . . something else?

Michael shrugs.

—You walked down from Atlanta, right? Were they everywhere you went? All the woods you've passed at night?

—Pretty much, Michael says, nodding.

—And?

—And what?

—What do you think they are?

—If the world were a different place, I'd really enjoying speculating about them, exploring what they might be, but with the way things are . . . with what I have to do . . . there is only . . . what has to be done. And right now that's walking as fast as we can. I'd really like to get to Marianna before nightfall.

—We can speculate and walk at the same time, can't we? Surely two urbane, sophisticated gents such as ourselves can do that. Make the time go by better.

Without warning, Michael lunges at the old man, knocking him to the ground and holding him there, soot and ash rising around them.

As Jackson runs back, Michael grabs him too.

Holding a finger over his lips to *shh* the old man, Michael points toward the road.

As the old man turns his head to see, the younger man pets the dog and holds his muzzle closed.

Out on the road a group of armed marauders passes by in a jacked-up redneck pickup truck complete with sexy girl silhouette mud flaps, Bondo and primer spots, and the yellow-and-black Gadsden flag bumper sticker, coiled, striking rattlesnake above the words DON'T TREAD ON ME.

Dirty. Desperate. Hungry. Hunting. Three men in the cab, four more on the back beneath the large confederate flag whipping in the wind. All white. All armed. All in combinations of camouflage and athletic attire.

The high-riding truck is black and chrome, its once shiny grill blackened with blood.

The truck is moving very slowly, but has obviously also been modified to run silently. Before the end, it would've had a glass pack or chambered or turbo muffler system to get the biggest, loudest, most beast-like roar to blast as it burned down the highway, but now sneak thieves need to be stealthy to stalk their unsuspecting prey.

This is the farthest south he's seen such a group and it surprises him, but it shouldn't. Nothing should.

If they hear us we're dead.

They don't have to hear you. They could see you.

The burned-out forest they're lying in offers very little in the way of cover, the blackened bodies of young pines narrow and bare, ashen understory thin and scraggly.

He's no match for the group of men, and the old man and the dog would only be liabilities in any engagement.

—Don't move a muscle, he whispers to Augustus. And help me keep the dog quiet.

If they can't keep the dog still and silent, he'll have to kill him, something he truly doesn't want to do.

From his prone position, Augustus pulls the dog to him, hugging him the way you would a frightened child.

Remaining as flat as possible, Michael reaches into the duffel and withdraws a rifle for the marauders and a knife for the dog.

Seeming to sense the seriousness of the situation, the dog stays silent and even appears to return Augustus's embrace.

The truck is moving so slow it seems as though it

will never pass.

Then it slows even further.

Don't stop. Don't stop. Please don't stop.

Then it stops.

To his surprise the vehicle is louder idling than it was while moving.

Though the truck is stationary, the flag continues to flap in the breeze, gray dust and debris rising off of it with every snap.

The old man holding the dog, the dog appearing to be holding the man right back, is as sad and pathetic as anything he's seen lately—save the creature in the dog collar who ran out of the back of the FedEx truck.

He thinks of Dawn, of how much he misses her, of how long it has been since he has held her. His need for her is entire and he trembles with the force of it.

No one gets out of the truck. And eventually it continues on, slowly down 73 toward 231.

6

The back of Augustus's head is bleeding.

The old man reaches up to it with the bent fingers of his misshapen hand. It's tender to the touch.

—Let me see it, Michael says.

—It's okay. I'm fine. Ready to move. Don't make a fuss. I ain't no soft little schoolgirl.

Michael grabs the man's head a little forcefully and turns the wound toward him. It's worse than he thought.

—Sit.

He helps the old man back down to the ground.

—I'm okay, Augustus says. No need for any of this.

Easing his duffels to the ground, Michael withdraws a small Mora axe and a Bushcraft survival knife and moves to the nearest pine tree.

Hacking away the charred bark, he notches out a small V-shaped incision into the deeper layer of the wood and waits.

As the pine resin begins to seep into the notch, he

slides the tip of his knife blade into it. Once the point of the knife is covered with sap, he steps back over to Augustus and smears the thick, sticky substance all over his wound.

—What's that gonna do? Augustus asks.

—Stem the blood flow, keep bacteria out, seal the wound.

—How d' you know that?

—Remembered a few things from research for an environmental thriller I wrote a while back, but not much. Read up on shit like that when all this started to go down. But I probably would've intuited this one. Raised rural. Come from a family of North Florida turpentiners. Grew up hearing all about the miraculous wonders of pine resin.

Augustus nods.

—But I can't do much more than that, so try not have any more injuries and no severe ones.

—Didn't *try* to have that one, he says. Could say I was just an innocent bystander who got bowled over.

7

Midday.

Brightest concentration of grayness directly over-head.

Moving. Slowly. Too slowly.

—The knife was for the dog, wasn't it? Augustus asks. You were going to slit its throat.

—Only if I had to.

—What about me?

—What about you?

—Would you have put me down too? the old man asks, his voice neutral, his tone expressing only mild inter-est.

—Not gonna do anything to anyone I don't have to. Not gonna let anything stop me from finding my family.

The old man nods and considers it.

—If you want to take the dog and go a different direction, I'll give you food and water.

The old man seems to consider it, but doesn't say

anything.

They walk in silence for a while, zigzagging in and out and around the trees on the fringe of the forest, staying out of sight of the road.

—What was Marianna like when you came through it? Michael asks.

—Didn't go through it. Came from Cottondale. Only saw a little of the destruction from a distance. But even from afar it was . . . I've never seen anything like it. Seems unreal. It's . . . it's total devastation. It's not like here either. Not hot and dry and ashy, but wet and cold. Like I said, I didn't see much. Heard some things, but CJ was the only living soul I saw.

They are walking along the edge of the woods, easing toward Marianna, Jackson trailing behind them, tethered to Augustus by a leash tied to a belt loop on his pants.

Both the old man and the dog are panting.

They have been walking for hours.

It's a slower pace than Michael would like. More risky too. Neither the old man nor the dog know how to be inconspicuous or quiet exactly.

It was a mistake to let them come with him.

—Hey neighbor, Augustus says. Mind if we stop and rest a minute? Have a little water.

—Movin' too slow as it is. Hate to stop.

The dog is straining against the leash, pulling at a pace the old man can't match. Several times he stumbles and almost falls as the animal lurches forward. It'd be better for him if Michael would take the leash, but he wants to keep his hand on the weapon and be ready to use it if the need arises.

—Okay. No problem. I's just a little worried about the pup. I'm fine. I keep trying to get him to pick up the pace, but . . .

Michael tries to figure out the best place to pause for water.

—Were you like this before? Augustus asks.

—Whatta you mean? Michael asks as he removes a

bottle of water from the duffel dangling beneath his right arm and hands it to him.

—This . . . wary. Guarded. Hardened. Driven.

Michael smiles.

—Actually, people remarked on my gentleness and kindness.

The old man tries to drink while walking, but can't quite negotiate the necessary steps.

Michael stops and calls Jackson back.

Augustus takes a big gulp from the bottle.

—That's why I asked, he says, wiping his mouth. It's still there. I can see some of it—underneath the . . . other.

Digging a small plastic bowl out of the duffel, Michael pours in a little water, which Jackson quickly laps up with his long tongue.

—Some of it comes from what I've experienced the past couple of months—and the way the world is now—but mostly it's the mission.

He thinks about roles and responsibilities.

He had been a kind and gentle soul, known for his belief in and commitment to love. But capable of confrontation, even force if called for.

This dichotomy was most pronounced in his role as protector of his children and wife.

A man of peace, who attempted to live his conviction of loving his enemies and blessing his cursers, he played a very different role in his responsibility as a father and husband.

He recalls something he used to tell his children when they were young, small, and vulnerable. Anybody truly ever hurts you, he had told them, I will hack them into little pieces.

This always elicited the same response, evoked the same reaction—*DAD!*

They didn't like hearing it, but neither did they doubt it.

—Finding your family? Augustus says.

—Doing all I can for them. It's what I've always

done as a husband, a dad. I won't resort to brutishness and I won't be aggressive or become like the inhumans, but to get to them, to protect them, to do my duty as a dad and a husband, I'll do what I have to.

Michael bends to give the animal a bit more water.

—The world's an abyss now, Augustus says. One that looks back at you when you look into it. Be careful not to become monstrous while dealing with the monsters of the new world.

—The world itself is a monster, Michael says.

—Which is why it's so easy to become one now. More than it ever was before.

The world had always been monstrous for some people. He realizes now he had judged those people and their response to their world too harshly.

—Always been more a monster for some than others. Even in the old world.

—That's a fact. But we're talking about you. You're guarded. And I understand where it comes from. What I'm sayin' is guard you heart, partner.

He nods.

—Thing is . . . part of the way you do it is to open it up. Get what I'm sayin'? One way you guard your heart is by being less guarded.

He nods again.

—Listen, neighbor, Augustus says. I can tell you know what I mean. So that's the end of my little reminder.

—Sorry if I seem harsh, but I've lost so much time already. I just feel like I . . . If I don't find them . . . Anyway, haven't quite gotten my legs under me yet. Still getting acclimated. Figured I'd figure it out once I finish what I have to do, but you're right. Been enough lost humanity already.

Augustus nods.

—I'm just trying to get home, Michael says.

He thinks of what spiritual teacher Ram Dass said— that we're all just walking each other home.

He's trying so hard to get home, feels such overwhelming pressure to do so, but if he can walk others to where they're going along the way, he should. It's the least he can do.

—Hate to say it, brother, Augustus says, but you have no home to walk home to. None of us do.

—My wife is my home. So are my kids. I have to find them. Nothing—

He starts to say nothing else matters, but that's not true. That's Augustus's point. Other things matter too—just not as much. Not nearly as much.

If I lose my self and my humanity, then I won't be able to be their home, the home they need me to be.

Everything matters or nothing does.

—What were you going to say? Augustus asks.

—Something that wasn't true. Thanks for the reminder. I needed to hear it. Appreciate you saying it. You able to walk some more now?

—I'm good to go. Thanks for the rest.

8

Four miles from Marianna.

Field.

Farm.

Frangible brown and gold grass dusted with gray.

Across the road from where they are awkwardly walking on the edge of the woods, the forest opens to reveal two empty, partially fenced pastures on either side of a long dirt driveway leading up to an old wooden farmhouse.

About halfway up the drive, a small, old, hunter-green Toyota pickup sits at an angle, its driver's side door open.

Augustus stops and looks over at it.

—Want to ride the rest of the way? he asks.

There are two reasons why Michael's used very few vehicles on his long journey. The first is he's useless when it comes to automobile mechanics. The second is using a vehicle attracts attention.

When the end began, when he realized what was happening and what it meant he'd have to do to find his family and save them if he could, bury and memorialize them if he couldn't, he had gone directly to the nearest Army Navy and Outdoor stores and gathered the supplies he would need—including a couple of books on survival.

While others watched and denied, he had acted.

After he was injured and while he was recuperating, he had read and reread the survival guides over and over, gathered more gear, and prepared himself as much as he possibly could.

What he had not done, what he had failed to do, was apply himself to learning anything at all about auto mechanics.

And though most vehicles he had encountered on his travels were out of gas or had dead batteries, there was nothing he could do if it was something else, even something minor.

Dawn could. Dawn would be better at all of this than him. They have different skill sets and hers are far more suited to survival. Not only had she been raised by a military dad in a rough and tumble way, but she had been both mom and dad to her only son, raising him in a similar manner. She had a bit of the brawler in her, wouldn't back down under any circumstances—from bar fights to bad boyfriends to the big bad world itself.

She often says being with him, having him love and care for and pamper her the way he does, has made her soft, but he knows it's not true, that the former fighter is still in her and would have come back out the moment the end began.

She has to be alive. She has to.

—Even if it has a little gas left, Michael says, I couldn't get it going.

—I can.

—You can?

—Old vehicle like that, piece of cake. Nothing to it.

He thinks about it, weighing whether it's worth attempting. Even if Augustus can get it running, the risks involved in actually driving it into town, of being so visible and vulnerable, are enormous. And if Augustus can't get it running, the diversion will not only waste valuable time but have had them unnecessarily exposed.

 —I don't know . . .

 —I can get it running.

 —I don't doubt that.

 —Then what?

He explains his hesitation.

 —What if you continue on while I go get the truck. I'll pick you up down the road.

 —And if it's out of gas or you can't get it running?

 —I won't have slowed you down any more and I'll catch up with you later or I won't. Hell, may even head in the other direction.

Michael thinks about it.

 —We go over and see if it's even feasible, he says. If you can get it going quickly, we do it, if not, we walk away fast, continue toward town, go even farther tonight to make up for the time we lose in the attempt.

9

Seen from a distance.
> Through a Bushnell Drop Zone scope.
> Two figures crossing the road.
> Some four hundred yards away.
> A man with a backpack carrying duffel bags. An old man spurred on by a lurching Lab and Catahoula mix at the end of the leash in his right hand.
> The small four dots beneath the intersection of the crosshairs move from figure to figure. Slowly. Lingering almost lovingly.

10

After carefully searching up and down the road, the two men and their mutt cross quickly, continuing to scan the area around them as they do.

Jogging down the dirt driveway, day fading fast, gray and white dust rising with every footfall.

The old man is looking at the truck. The younger man is looking everywhere else.

Duffels and backpack heavy. Shoulders, neck, and back sore, strained, aching. Hurting worse as he looks over his shoulder, searches the road, scans the low, gray horizon.

Some twenty feet beyond the vehicle, the black liquid stain of a once living being. Remnants of a rotting corpse.

The truck is tiny, its cab and bed filled with clutter.

Inside, food containers, junk mail, cups, shoes, random tools, papers, trash, farm equipment catalogs.

On the back, electric fence wire, galvanized and PVC pipe, shovel, rake, flower pot, sewer snake, chains, bungees, random strands of dried-out hay, aluminum cans.

—Be dark soon, Michael says. Don't have much time to make it work.

Augustus climbs in and gives it a try.

The little vehicle sounds for a second like it's going to start, but doesn't.

Popping the hood, the old man begins to fiddle around with the engine as Michael removes binoculars from his bag and begins to glass the flatlands surrounding them.

Ashen landscape, bits of it drifting around like large dirty dust motes.

The pastures are bordered on three sides by woods, the fourth, the front, by what's left of the missing, leaning, and fallen fence, and the highway beyond.

Nothing stirs along the road.

On the far horizon, trees sway and twitch, but he can't tell if someone or something is in them or if it's just the work of the wind.

He quickly scans either side of the stand and comes back to it, straining to see beyond the burned-out tree line, but the distance is too great, the late afternoon light too gray for him to see anything much more than movement.

—We need to go, he says, still scanning the area.

—Think I almost got it. Give me another second.

This time on his sweep of the area, he sees a curtain move in the little farmhouse farther up the drive.

—Time's up, he says.

—Climb in and give it a try, Augustus says.

He does.

—Moment of truth, Michael says as he pushes in the clutch and turns the key.

The ignition turns over, then ticks but doesn't start.

He pats the accelerator a few times and tries again.

The little engine gives a series of gurgling growls, coughs, sputters, and then it starts.

—Hurry. Get in. Let's go.

Leaving the truck cranked, Michael jumps out, removes his backpack and grabs the duffels and slings them in the back, withdraws a weapon, and climbs back into the small cab to find both Jackson and Augustus waiting for him.

Putting the truck in gear, he pulls forward to turn around, the entire vehicle shimmying as he attempts to figure out the best gas-to-clutch ratio.

He heads in the wrong direction for a while before finding an area big enough to turn around. When he finally does, his turn is slow and awkward and the little truck jerks and spits and sputters.

Jackson readjusts often to find his footing.

Augustus sits in silence, worn out from the earlier exertion.

The spot in the drive big enough to turn around is only twenty feet or so from the farmhouse, and Jackson begins to bark at it, then whine and whimper.

What the hell is in there?

As they begin to race away, back down the dirt drive toward the road that will take them into town, he glances in the rearview mirror, placing a hand on the cowering animal as he does. There in the grimy, soot-speckled reflection, he sees what he believes to be a frightening figure in the upstairs window.

Tapping his brakes for a better look, he sees in the faintest of flashes the misshapen form before it vanishes back behind the curtain. There bathed in the blood-red brake light, something that may once have been human hunches its dramatically uneven shoulders and bends its malformed head to peer after them with a single nearly completely hooded eye.

Inhuman, yet terribly too human, it was as horrific a face as he'd yet encountered in this new nightmare the world had awakened into.

11

—I was some help after all, Augustus says.

   —A big help, Michael responds.

   They are driving the last few miles of Highway 73 in the gray gloaming, lights off, moving slowly, attempting to be as inconspicuous as possible.

   If only the tiny truck were gray instead of green.

   Jackson has stopped whimpering but lies deathly still in the seat, looking up at the two men with shy, anxious eyes.

   —Beats hell outta walkin', Augustus adds.

   As if a commercial airliner crash site, the road is a long, dense debris field that only increases and intensifies as they near the city.

   Vehicles litter the road of course, but bicycles and wagons and strollers too.

   Cast off clothes. Trunks. Suitcases.

   Plastic storage containers. Plastic bags. Plastic dishes. Plastic pots and pans.

Overturned shopping carts.

Books. Magazines. All manner of media—records, CDs, DVDs, tapes.

Electronics. TVs. Computers. Laptops. Monitors. Radios. Boom boxes. Tablets.

Things that used to have value that have value no more.

He weaves the small Toyota in and out and around the abandoned cars and fallen trees, and avoids all the other items as much as possible, but there's so much of it, much of it crunching beneath the small tires.

—Where're we headed first? Augustus asks.

—My daughter, Meleah, was at Marianna High School for training when all the clocks stopped. Headed there now, but first gonna make a quick stop by my good friend Lynn's house. It's on the way. Want to check on him and his family. He's not only one of the very best friends I've ever had, but his daughter is my son's girlfriend.

The old man nods.

—He's very, very smart and capable. Has lived all over the world. Was in the military. College professor with a wealth of knowledge. If he survived the initial fallout, he'll still be alive.

—Doesn't mean he'll still be here. Think most survivors are long gone.

—Hope they all are—including Meleah, but I have to check.

Suddenly, seemingly out of nowhere, something hits the back right quarter panel hard.

Michael speeds up, the little truck lurching forward.

—The hell was that? Augustus asks, stiffly turning to see.

Muffled moans erupt from the area.

In the rearview mirror, Michael sees a tall man on a small bicycle in only dingy white underwear, boots, and an antique leather bird beak gas mask with built-in goggles.

Peddling fast, he's attempting to catch up to them, yelling something from within the beak of his mask as he does.

—There a psyche ward around here I don't know about? Augustus asks. Or you think his crazy ass came over from Chattahoochee?

Jackson had begun to whimper again.

Michael attempts to pat him while driving.

Lights on now. Going too fast not to have them, though the illumination they provide is scant at best.

—He's gaining on us, Augustus says. Can't you go any faster?

—Not without hitting something.

Augustus turns and studies the man some more.

—Doesn't look like he's armed.

—Doesn't have to be, Michael says. Probably has crazy retarded strength.

Peddling like a maniac, the man comes up beside them and lunges—leaping into the back of the bed with Michael's supplies and weapons. Not to mention all the other things that can be used as weapons.

Michael stomps on the brakes and the bird man falls forward fast, slamming into the back of the cab hard.

Jamming the truck into neutral and jerking up the emergency brake, he jumps out and brings his short shotgun up to level it at the disturbing creature trying to climb to his feet.

The man raises the mask to the top of his head to reveal a soft, pale early twenties man with a sparse blond beard and wild blue eyes.

—Fuck hell you do that for, dude? You some sort of for real fucktard?

—Why'd you jump in the back of our truck?

—'Cause you wouldn't stop and I had to warn you.

—Warn us about what?

—The crater. You'd'a run right into it and died. You'd be dead right now instead of interrogating me with a rifle.

—It's a shotgun.

—Whatever, man. Who the fuck cares what it is?

—Two people. The one doing the shooting and the one being shot at. What crater?

—Why don't you have any pants on? Augustus asks. You're frightening our dog.

—*Your* dog. *Your* truck. Looks like the Thompson's little farm truck and that fat fuck son of a bitch Frank Fuckin' Friedman's dog to me.

—What crater?

—The one you were about to drive off into. Right there in the middle of the motherfuckin' road.

—Weren't even driving fast until your crazy bird ass started chasing us, Augustus says.

Michael looks at Augustus.

—You were just here earlier today, right? You'd know if there was a big ass crater in the road.

—We cut through the woods.

—That was retarded, the bird man says. Only thing more dangerous than the road is the woods.

—Came out further down along the road. Didn't see this section.

—Get down out of the truck, Michael says to the bird man, using the shotgun to indicate the way. Slowly.

—I ain't about getting my ass shot. Just be cool, bro.
He climbs down.

—Show us this crater.

—Will you thank me and suck my dick if I do?

—If you truly kept us from falling to our fiery deaths, Augustus says, we'll thank you, sure enough, but that's the best deal you're gonna get from any of us. Including the dog.

He leads them to a place about fifteen feet away where the highway comes to an abrupt end, falling away so fast and so far down that the bottom is not visible.

Fifty feet across and at least that wide, the gulf bisects the highway with a big black hole.

—You're welcome, the bird man says.

—Thank you, Michael says.

—Even closer than I thought. Y'all were goners for

sure.

He may have been able to stop in time, but it's dark enough and difficult enough to see that he would have most likely driven off into it—especially at the speed he was going to try to get away from the bird man.

—What made you warn us? Michael asks.

He looks confused.

—Because it was there, dude. I don't know. Whatta you mean?

—Never did say why you don't have any pants on, Augustus says.

—Wasn't expecting company, man. I don't know. I don't dig pants. Whatta you want me to say?

—And what's up with that bird mask?

—It's the only mask I could find. And I find it groovy dude. Don't you? Beak is stuffed with cotton and cloth. Filters my air before I breathe it. You ain't seen all that shit floating around? Can't be good for us.

—Ain't much left that's good for us, Augustus says.

—I was gonna offer you a ride back to your bike, Michael says.

—Yeah?

—But you can just take the truck. It's no good to us anymore.

—Wow. Really man? You're gonna give me someone else's truck that's no use to you anymore? You're like the most generous motherfucker ever.

—You need some food and water?

—Wouldn't say no to it. You have some?

—Where do you live? How are you surviving here?

—There's nothin' here. Now that I have a truck, I'll throw my bike in the back and drive as far north as it will take me. Y'all should turn around too. Hell, y'all can even ride in the back of my truck with my bike if you like. I'm kidding. The three of us can fit in the front if the dog is in the back.

Michael turns to Augustus.

—You and Jackson could go with him, he says. The

air is a little better and the—

—Always tryin' to get rid of me, the old man says. Now you're pawnin' me off on a man who doesn't wear pants.

—Hell, I'll put on some pants if it means that much to you. Let's go. Road trip. It'll be fun. You, me, and the mutt.

—I helped with the truck, Augustus says to Michael. May be of some more help still. Jackson and I are sticking with you.

—Then it's settled. Need to keep moving. Been here too long already.

12

Destruction. Devastation. Ruination.

The main drag of Marianna is decimated.

Buildings flattened. Trees and vehicles and light poles in the road. Many structures missing completely.

The sheer scale of the catastrophic leveling of the little town is astonishing.

It's too far inland, of course, but it appears that the motherfucker of all hurricanes had hammer-punched the life out of the little town, pounding it without pity long after it was already dead and gone.

Huge chunks of highway missing.

The city's enormous water tower toppled and tuberous, its massive steel structure spread across the highway like bleached dinosaur bones, its tank now oblong.

Entire buildings lifted and dropped across the street intact. Other structures flung apart, their splintered wood looking like piles of matchsticks.

What trees are left are filled with debris—awnings,

rooftops, billboards, even entire vehicles. A stand of oak trees holds a semi tractor-trailer some fifty feet in the air.

Damp.

Cold.

Dreary.

Unlike the area he has just traveled through, there is no ash here. Everything is damp and wet and soggy, and the temperature has dropped twenty degrees.

Gas stations gone.

Their tanks tossed to and fro, their sides gashed open.

Overturned oil trucks.

The surface of the water on the roads and sidewalks and the foundations of former buildings is slick with gas and oil, swirls of periwinkle, magenta, violet, goldenrod that remind him of the inside of an oyster shell.

Michael finds an overturned newspaper box and sets one of his duffels on it. Unzipping it, he withdraws a tightly folded coat for himself and a poncho for Augustus.

—Much obliged, the old man says, shivering as he shimmies into the warmer garment.

—All the surfaces are going to be slick, Michael says. Be careful.

Before zipping up the bag, he withdraws a weapon, a Smith .45 automatic. After double-checking the safety, he shoulders the duffel and they continue.

They walk slowly down Highway 90, weaving, twisting, turning, negotiating around everything as if in a hoarder's attic.

Every sound arises from wind and water.

The breeze in their ears. Brisk. Cold. Whining.

The drip and splash and run of water.

All of which makes it seem even colder than it is.

Somewhere in the dim distance the chord on a flagpole clangs desultorily.

Clang. Clang. Clang.

Up ahead is the Waffle House where he had met his daughter Meleah for breakfast on that last morning, when he was headed to Atlanta and she was in town for training at the high school. Just a quick cup of coffee and some toast for her, a Diet Coke and hash browns and bacon for him. Nothing special. But the conversation—their conversations were always special. Even when they weren't about anything particularly special. As usual they spoke about what they were reading and the latest show they were binging on, but just as usual their conversation included how they were really doing—what they were dealing with, what life was attempting to teach them.

His final words to her, hers to him, were the same as they were to all his loved ones, his family and friends. The phrase he had said more than any other over his decades on this planet, the one he had purposed to be the final one he'd ever say to them, though he now hopes more than anything those were not his final words to her.

So proud of you. Love you so much.

Love you, Dad.

He can't quite make out the Waffle House, but it looks altered and oddly shaped somehow.

A little closer and he sees why.

As they near the Rahal Chevrolet dealership, he can see that not a single vehicle is left on the lot, and several are piled on the flattened Waffle House across the street. Down the way, Chipola Ford looks much the same.

—Almost dark, Augustus says. Need to find shelter soon.

—I think we can make it to Lynn's.

—No way to know if it's even there. Doesn't look like much of anything is left around here.

—Come on. Let's cut through here.

They head down Milton Avenue, a side street between an Assembly of God church with only a sign and one wall left standing and a McDonald's with only a single giant golden arch and a drive thru order board remaining.

Milton leads down a quarter mile or so then turns to the right and becomes Kelson—the street Lynn's house is on about a mile down the way.

Trees, power lines, and light poles are down. Doors and shudders and shingles, boards and vinyl siding litter the street, but many of the houses are still mostly intact, and the debris is nothing compared to that out on Highway 90.

They can move much more quickly now. And do. At least at first. Then . . .

The last of the gray light leaves the world and the two men and the mutt are left in utter darkness.

Jackson begins to whimper.

—Whatta we do now? Augustus says.

Pausing for a moment, Michael withdraws another weapon and two flashlights, handing one of the lights and the other weapon to Augustus.

—Should've given you a gun sooner, Michael says. Sorry.

Then the noises begin.

Not as feral, tortured, guttural, or as concentrated here as in the woods, but every bit as disturbing.

Jackson cowers and begins to crawl on his belly—first in one direction then another.

—We're exposed out here, Augustus says.

—On three, click on our lights, take a quick look around, click them off, move to the opposite side of the road, and continue for another ten feet or so.

—We should do it standing back to back so we can see both ways, Augustus says. Make sure nobody's coming up behind us.

—Good thinking.

They move this way for a while, occasionally walking into or tripping over something, and make slow but certain progress down Kelson.

They are in the midst of this process in the pitch blackness when something darts in front of them in the street.

They sense the movement, of course, and hear something, but it is mostly that they feel the wind wake it causes.

Both men snap on their lights immediately, but nothing is there.

Jackson whimpers and whines and wets the already damp pavement beneath him.

—The hell was that? Augustus asks.

—Let's leave our lights on, Michael says. You walk straight, keeping an eye on what's in front of us and to our right. I'll back up behind you and watch behind and to the left. If anything rushes us just yell the direction.

—Okay.

They do this for a while and it seems to be working, and though they can still hear the nightmarish noises all around them, they don't see anything and nothing rushes them.

As they near the entrance to Chipola College at the intersection that is less than an eighth of a mile from Lynn's house, Augustus slows.

—What is it? Michael asks.

—See for yourself. Spin around. I'll take the back.

Michael comes around to the front to see a beige and yellow doublewide mobile home on its side blocking the entire street.

—Let's go around it. We're almost there.

—Following you.

They ease around the left side of the trailer toward Chipola College, walking where the sign used to be and now stands a partially collapsed batting cage.

Michael strains to see the campus, but nothing is visible. Just more blackness.

Movement inside the trailer.

Rattling. Large heavy object falling. Something shattering.

Back on Kelson. Moving faster now.

—Keep your eye on the trailer, Michael says.

—I'm watching everything. Just go.

Three houses. A drainage ditch with a guardrail along a wooded area, and then they're there.

Lynn's house.

Obliterated.

Reddish-orange bricks in rubble.

It looks like it's part of a war-torn village in Europe during World War II.

—Is that it? Augustus asks.

—Yeah.

—Sorry.

Michael begins moving toward the ruins.

—What're you doin'? Augustus asks. We've got to find shelter.

—I've got to take a closer look, got to be sure there's—

—I know he was your friend, but . . . there's nothing left to look at. We're too exposed out here like this. What happened to the guy who cared more about the mission than—

—This *is* the mission. Just give me a minute. Please.

Movement in the wooded area to the right.

Both men spin in that direction, guns up, the weak beams of their small flashlights only catching the rustling of a few tree branches.

—We need to find an abandoned house or even a vehicle, Augustus says. Anything to get out of the night.

—Okay. You're right. Let's go.

They turn to walk back down the driveway toward Kelson, when they hear it.

—Help me. Somebody please help me.

13

—**P**lease. Help me.

The cries for help are barely audible, just a decibel or two above a whisper.

A young female. Ragged. Hoarse. Harsh. Desperate.

Jackson begins to bark.

—Quiet boy, Augustus says.

—Please. Somebody.

The voice sounds like it could be that of Gracie—Lynn's youngest daughter and Michael's son Micah's girlfriend. Bouncing around a bit, carried by the wind, lost in the whine of the other noises, it seems to be coming from the wooded lot.

Michael starts that way, shrugging off his duffels as he does.

—Wait, Augustus says. It could be a trap. It could be . . . anything. We just don't know.

—It sounds like Lynn's daughter. I've got to—

—Okay, but let's at least—

—Somebody. Please.

Michael tucks the .45 in his waistband and withdraws the short shotgun from one of the duffels.

Jackson pulls on the lead in Augustus's hand, lunging toward the woods.

—He's ready, Michael says. You could let him go and we could follow him. Or you can come in behind me or from a different spot. Up to you, but I'm going now.

Without waiting for a response, Michael takes off, the beam of his flashlight bounding along the ground like a Follow the Bouncing Ball Song.

Before he reaches the woods, Jackson runs past him. Barking. Yelping.

Glancing over his shoulder, he sees that Augustus, moving slowly and stiffly, isn't far behind.

Unable to enter the woods where Jackson does, Michael finds a small opening close by and presses in, wet leaves smacking him on the face as he does.

Blacker than black. Darker than dark.

The wet woods are a shade of night he's never seen.

He scans the area with the beam of his flashlight, holding it on the barrel of the shotgun so they move together.

Pines. Poplars. Oaks. Kudzu. The woods, which surround a drainage conduit large enough to walk in that passes beneath the road, run all the way to the Chipola River.

He can see nothing but the beam, nothing but the slightly less blackness inside the small circle of impotent illumination.

He strains to hear Jackson and attempts to follow the sound as best he can.

The ground is damp and his boots slide, unable to secure any traction, and he slips often but manages to stay on his feet.

Soon the slick surface is slanting down, falling off fast.

Feet out from underneath him. Falling. Hitting the ground hard. Holding onto gun and light. Sliding. Tumbling.

Thwack.

He hits the base of a pine tree hard and comes to an abrupt stop.

Can't . . . breathe. Air . . . won't . . . enter.

Eventually he gets a big gulp of air.

As soon as he can, he yells up to Augustus.

—STEEP INCLINE. STOP. STAY UP—

—I'm good, Augustus says. Saw you tumble and put on the brakes. You okay?

Jackson lets out a yelp and begins to cry.

The disembodied girl's voice screams.

Both come from the backside of the lot.

Michael scurries to his feet and heads in that direction. Twenty feet above him, Augustus heads the same way.

More screams.

Jackson starts barking again, but then yelps in pain.

Running.

Blind.

Buffeted by branches and undergrowth and trees—standing and fallen—and kudzu. Everywhere kudzu.

Stumbling. Tripping.

Limbs. Twigs. Branches. Snapping. Crunching. Popping.

Now that they're being noisy, Michael pulls out the .45, thumbs the safety off and the hammer back, and fires a round into the air.

This act causes him to collide with an oak tree, scraping his cheek and dazing him slightly.

He doesn't stop. Tries not to even slow.

Gaining ground.

Jackson's barking. Gracie's screams. Closer. Much closer.

As he makes his way toward the noises, his flashlight plays across the forest floor.

Tracks. Footprints.

Then feet.

Bare feet. Light moving up. Following tattered trousers, torn shirt.

Seen in quick flashes.

Contorted face. Blood streaked. Teeth snarling. Guttural growling sounds. Eyes that seem to glow but be dead somehow.

Split-second assessment.

Threat.

React.

He squeezes the trigger.

Blast.

The loud explosion momentarily silences all the other noises around him.

The man is gone.

He shines the light at the ground, then all around him.

Nobody. No blood. Nothing. Had he imagined it? Is he seeing things?

Continuing.

—You okay? Augustus yells.

—Yeah. See anything?

—Look.

He shines his light up. About ten feet in front of him, Gracie hanging from a zip line, kicking at a man trying to grab her feet as Jackson nips at him.

Augustus's bouncing beam of light lets Michael know he's making his way down the embankment.

Gracie dangles from a zip line attached to a treehouse some twenty-five yards back and twenty feet up in a large oak tree.

The man after her reminds him of the one he has just encountered. Something about the way he moves and looks and sounds. If he weren't dressed differently, if it weren't impossible, he'd believe it's the same man.

He aims low to avoid hitting Gracie and to the left to avoid hitting Jackson, but Augustus fires first.

Like before, nothing is there. Nothing is hit.

—Scan the area and cover us, Michael says. I'm gonna help her down.

He rushes over to Gracie.

—*Michael?* she says in shock. What are you— Is Micah with you?

He helps her down.

—No. Have you seen him since . . . since the end?

—No.

She is small and thin—even thinner than before—and weighs next to nothing. Her blond hair is damp and matted. Her face streaked with sweat and tears and fear.

—What about Meleah? Michael asks. I was hoping she might come find you guys when all this started. She was at the high school for training.

—I know. I saw her there. We were supposed to have lunch, but the woman doing the training was killed in a car accident on the way to it. The training was canceled. Meleah left early.

—You sure?

—Positive.

Augustus comes up.

—How the hell did I miss? he says.

—Fuckers are fast, Gracie says. They're . . .

—Gracie, Augustus, Michael says. Augustus, Gracie.

—Nice to meet you, ma'am.

—Come on, Michael says. We've got to go. Where's your dad?

—He went scavenging this afternoon. He should've been back before dark. Something's wrong. I was going to look for him. So stupid, but I didn't know what else to do. Dog saved my life.

—Good boy, Jackson, he said, patting the dark near where he thinks the animal is.

—I think he's hurt.

—We'll look after him, but we've got to find a safe place to—

—In the treehouse, she says. It's safe. Come on. We can look for Dad at first light.

—Who were those men? Michael asks.

—Just some of the many bad ones running loose

across the land these days. Come on.

—How many are there? How persistent are they?

She leads them over to the large oak that holds the treehouse.

The two men scan the area around them with their lights, their weapons out and up. Ready.

Jackson, moving slowly, follows along behind them emitting a low whine.

—My dad started this for me when I was little. Finished it after the . . . after what happened.

The large tree has no low branches and there is no ladder.

—How do you—

Before he can finish, Gracie does something in the darkness he can't see and a rope ladder falls down from the treehouse.

—You able to climb that? he asks Augustus.

—You damn skippy, he says. Even if I couldn't, I'd figure out a way. Sure as shit ain't stayin' down here.

—You two go up, then I'll carry Jackson. Then I've got to go get my bags.

—We've got a lift we can put Jackson on, Gracie says. I'll lower it when I get up there. It's a counterweighted pulley system Dad designed. I can pull him up no problem.

14

With Gracie, Augustus, and Jackson secure in the treetops, and the rope ladder up there with them, Michael makes his way back to Lynn's front yard, hoping his duffels with his supplies are still there.

Gun drawn. Light on. Looking over his shoulder often. Pausing occasionally, using the bases of tress for cover. Scanning the area around him.

It's so dark and he's so tired.

His cheek hurts from hitting the tree, but mostly his neck and shoulders and back hurt from the way the backpack and duffels are wrecking his body.

He had chosen to leave his backpack in the tree-house. Was that a mistake?

Where is Lynn? What's happened to him? Something bad or he'd be back. No way he'd leave Gracie alone after dark if he was physically able to make it back.

Instead of walking back through the woods the way he came, he makes his way toward the slope, climbs up it, out of the woods, then across Lynn's backyard to come up beside the rubble to the front.

He pauses at the side of the house, now just a pile of bricks, and scans the entire area—the yard, the street, the edge of the woods.

The duffels are still there.

Not much good has happened since the end arrived, but finding his duffels still on Lynn's lawn ranks high on that short list.

As he nears them, he sees that one is partially un-zipped. Had he left it that way or has someone been in it?

Looking around, he quickly kneels down to check them.

He can't even begin to do what he needs to without the contents of these two bags.

Everything seems to be here.

As he's zipping the bag back up, he senses someone coming up behind him, moving awkwardly.

He tucks and rolls over into a sitting position, bring-ing up the shotgun as he does.

Blood-covered. Clothes and face and glasses splat-tered. Machete held down at his side still wet, dripping.

Lynn.

Slowly staggering toward him on a makeshift crutch hacked out of a tree branch. Canvas backpack draped over his left shoulder, machete in his right hand.

Embattled. In very bad shape. Barely able to move. Limping severely.

He attempts to hold up his hands. Neither rises much.

—Don't shoot.

Part 2
Night Fires of the New World

1

Slowly.

So very slowly.

He helps his injured friend across the yard, past the rubble remnants of the house he once called home, down the slope of damp dirt and coiling, climbing kudzu vines, through the dense, dark forest, to the treehouse he had started so long ago for amusement and had so recently finished for sanctuary.

—The men who attacked Gracie, Michael says. Who are they? Will they be back tonight? Can they get into the treehouse?

—We'll be safe up there. They're . . . I'm not exactly sure what they are. I'm not certain there's much that's human left in them. They've been altered by . . . something. Infection? Radiation? Maybe it's just trauma.

—Seems like more.

—Whatever it is . . . they can't climb.

The ladder is dropped down by a grateful daughter.

And together they climb.
Rung by rung.
Slowly.
Gingerly.
Lynn's arm around Michael's shoulder, his wounded leg dangling down. Both men pulling up with all their might.

Stretch and strain and creak of rope and wood.
—It will hold, Lynn says, his soft voice prayerful.
Michael nods. Takes a breath. Continues.
Beyond depleted. Beyond drained. Utterly wrung out.

Reserve strength. Reserve energy.
No way he's not accomplishing this one last task for today. Helping lift his friend to safety.
The arduous, precarious process calls to mind a poem Lynn wrote many, many years before called *The Heavy Lifting*.

In the insightful poem, Lynn lifts his young daughters, carrying them from car to bed after they fall asleep on the way home. He injures his back lifting a drunk paraplegic vet who has fallen out of his wheelchair. He reflects on not lifting his father at the end, how that task fell to strangers, paramedics.

Random lines come to mind.

Men can lift things, heavy things,
can on average run faster, longer
but have advantage in little else.
I wonder what all the lifting
will come to, how little it
has to do finally with being
a man, though it seems so
important at the time.

By the time they reach the top, their bags are waiting there for them.

Water. Food. Medicine. Supplies.

Augustus, who has spent a lifetime doing such things to farm animals, sets Lynn's broken leg.

Lynn passes out from the pain, Gracie from the sight of it.

—I was wrong about you, Michael says to Augustus. I'm sorry.

—May take me a while to get somewhere, Augustus says with an extra twinkle in his eye, but by god I'm worth the wait.

—Yes you are. You're far more suited to this world than I am, far more useful.

—You're doing just fine.

2

Small spartan space. Up above the fray. Cardboard boxes. Random canned goods. Bottled water. Depleted first-aid kit. Unlit Coleman lantern. Burning candles. A few books and keepsakes.

Sleep.

Dreams.

Four humans—three men and a young woman. One animal—a very brave Catahoula Lab mix named for Florida's first military governor.

Inside—snoring, breathing, mumbling. Outside— unearthly sounds from down below.

Waking.

Flickering candlelight.

An open book lying across his chest. Ron Hansen's *Mariette in Ecstasy*. He holds it like a lover.

Augustus, supposed to be on watch, is fast asleep.

Seeing Lynn rousing.

Administering water and more pain pills from his pack.

—Thank you, Lynn says.

Michael shakes his head.

—How're you feeling?

—A lot better. Gracie okay?

—Yeah. Just been through a lot from the looks of it.

—All have, Lynn says.

—Did you think we'd ever witness a world like this?

—Seemed inevitable.

He often thinks the earth is merely fighting a toxic infection that just happens to be the virus of humanity.

—We reaped the whirlwind, Michael says.

—It's what happens when you sow the wind.

—Sudden, once it started, once we breached the brink.

Jackson sniffles and snorts and adjusts his bandaged body.

—What're y'all still doing here? Michael asks.

—Gracie's been sick, unable to travel. Too dangerous anyway. Joy's in Tallahassee—or was when it happened. Jill was over there too, but they weren't together. I've wanted to go there and to Panama City to check on my mom, but . . . have been unable to do either. And they say Blountstown is completely underwater now, impassable.

—We'll figure out our next steps tomorrow. Get some sleep.

—What book do you have?

He tells him.

—Have another? Lynn asks.

—Of course. Would you like *A Widow for One Year*, *The Hours*, *Oracle Night*, *Open Secret*, *Rabbit Run*?

—Surprise me.

He hands him *Mariette in Ecstasy*.

The book is received in the same manner it is given. Carefully. Reverentially. Like two curators handling the last known art object of its kind.

—Either they no longer matter at all, Lynn says, or they matter more than they ever did before.

—I'm giving myself permanent back, shoulder, and

neck issues because I believe it's the latter.
          —Thanks for that. For this. Glad you're here. It's good to see you again.
          —You too.

3

Morning.

He's had very little sleep.

Spent the solitary hours of the night thinking, figuring, planning.

—I've been trying to figure out what to do next, Michael says softly, his mouth dry.

Only Lynn and Augustus are awake and he's trying not to disturb Gracie and Jackson.

—Come up with anything? Augustus asks.

—Gracie said Meleah left before everything started, he says. I have no way of knowing where she was headed or if she got there before it all began. I need to continue toward Wewa.

Lynn nods.

—But you can't travel and won't be able to do much for a while.

—Doesn't matter, Lynn says. You've got to look for her. Find her and the others.

—I think I might have a plan.

Michael turns to Augustus.

—Would you be willing to stay here for a while and help Lynn and Gracie? he asks. I'd leave food, water, and weapons for y'all.

—I'll be up and around in no time, Lynn says. There's no need—

—I'd be happy to, Augustus says.

—I was thinking I could go to Wewa and help get whoever's still alive out, then come back here. That'd give you time to heal. Then we'd figure out how to get to Panama City and Tallahassee.

—You've got to go, Lynn says. But you can't leave supplies and your partner behind. We'll—

—All I do is slow him down, Augustus says.

—All he does is slow me down, Michael says, smiling at Augustus.

—I *want* to stay, Augustus adds. You kidding. You have a house—a shelter to sleep in. My old bones much prefer this to walking fifty miles in treacherous, hostile, toxic territory. Let me stay. Please. You'd be doing me a favor.

Foraging.
Gathering.
More heavy lifting.
Preparing.
Securing.
Thinking. Always thinking.
Is this the right the thing to do? If not, what is? How can I know?

Both men know this could be the last time they ever see each other.

—I'm so glad I got to see you, Michael says.

He has spent much of the morning foraging for food and getting them set up with everything they need to survive.

They're in good shape and its far safer here than what he's about to attempt, but he still feels conflicted.

—Your friendship has meant more to me than you'll ever know, Lynn says.

Michael blinks a few times.

—I hope to be back in less than a week, he says. But I feel bad for leaving.

—We'll be fine. You've seen to that. Just look out for yourself out there.

Michael nods.

—Everything is different now, Lynn says. Everything. Don't hesitate. Deliberation was for the other world. Now there is only time to act. Don't hesitate to do what needs to be done. Find your family. Get them out of there.

—Thanks.

He steps over and hugs Gracie.

—Find Micah for me, she says. Bring him back with you.

—I will.

He moves toward the hatch.

Augustus opens it and drops down the rope ladder.

—Couldn't've done this without your help, Michael says. So glad we met up on the road. Thank you for everything.

—It was a grand adventure. I look forward to others with you.

—Take good care of them.

—Count on it. Just hurry back so you can see for yourself just how good.

4

Alone.

Again.

He had adjusted to having the companionship of Augustus and Jackson, and is now adjusting back.

He likes the silence and solitude. Has always needed a healthy dose of both to maintain a certain equilibrium and serenity.

Of course, recently he had been alone far too much—an experience that has left him emotionally raw-boned and psychologically susceptible.

Outside of Marianna.

Highway 73 heading toward home.

It had taken him a while to get through the wreckage of the crash site–like city. It's afternoon and he's made very little forward progress.

Up ahead the interstate overpass rises up above the road, suspended over I-10 below. There are no onramps, no access to the other road, only a bridge that avoids an actual intersection.

The day is less gray, the temperature marginally

warmer.

Unlike back in town, this strip of rural road is free of debris.

Untouched. Unscathed. Spared from all that has befallen so much of the area right around it.

Eerily empty, it appears to be abandoned.

He had wanted, even needed some silence and solitude—or thought he had—but perhaps, because of all he'd experienced lately, it isn't what he needs just now. Something deep inside him hums with the dull ache of loneliness.

Seeing Lynn had been so good; leaving him so difficult. Will he see his friend again? What about his other friends? Dave? Aaron? Dan? Lou? Herbie and Stacy?

His misses Dawn and his children more than he ever thought possible.

It eats away at him, hollowing him out inside. How long before he completely caves in from the cavernous hole at his empty center?

He finds climbing the incline of the overpass easier than he expects, realizes how much lighter his load is now, and is reminded he needs to find water, food, and medicine when he can. Stopping to scavenge will slow him down some, but not doing it is not an option.

In addition to some of his food and water, he left one of his shotguns, ammunition for it and for the pistol Lynn already had, a couple of his books, medicine, and medical supplies.

He doesn't have to replace everything he left behind, but certain items are absolutely essential.

At the top of the overpass, he pauses to look in both directions down I-10. Like this part of 73, it's utterly, absolutely, entirely empty.

No vehicles. No debris. No people. No animals. Nothing for as far as he can see.

It looks like a vanishing.

Though the destruction is more devastating to see, more frightening to comprehend, the desolate stretches are by far the more disturbing.

It's as if he's the last person on the planet. And he feels like he is.

He glances up at the gray sky above.

He assumes there is still a sun and that what remains of it is beyond the low slate ceiling, but all he can see is a faint gray glow diffused by something akin to charcoal smog. As usual, there are no birds. No direct sunlight. No clouds.

Here. In this place. There is also no wind. No sound. Still. Static. Stationary. Silent.

Nothing stirs. Nothing moves. Nothing makes a noise.

Uncanny. Unearthly. Vacuous.

There have been times in his life when he has been overcome by loneliness, when the core of him is gripped by a dull ache that feels like it's suffocating his soul.

He experiences this type of utter emptiness as a kind of ultimate absence, a vacancy, a void not unlike the lonely landscape he's in right now.

This place is deserted, abandoned, forsaken, and that's exactly how he feels.

Vacuity. Nullity. Nothingness.

The empty abyss inside him is as unforgivingly untenanted as the world about him, and in this moment he wonders if he'll ever again encounter another living soul, if, in fact, he's any longer a living soul himself.

Encounter is one thing. Truly connect is another. Will he ever again experience the ecstasy of intimacy?

Of course you won't. You're a fool on a fool's errand. There is no one waiting on you, no one living left behind. You're walking directly to your death, you dumb motherfucker.

Well, then let's get on with it.

He starts walking again. Faster this time. Almost running.

Can't outrun loneliness. It's in you, and you can't outrun yourself.

5

In addition to leaving Lynn and the others a weapon, ammunition, medical supplies, food and water, he had also given them his can opener and one of his three remaining LifeStraws.

He needs to stop and restock. He especially needs to find another can opener.

Not far from the overpass, he comes to a small area with a little development along the road. Four or five places on either side of the highway. A few houses. A few mobile homes. A random roadside business or two. A small farm with a still standing fence but no livestock inside it.

The area is open. Mostly yards. Very little cover.

One corner between two of the lots has a few trees and bushes. He ducks in them, withdraws his binoculars, waits, and watches.

There are no vehicles in any of the driveways.

No movement in or around any of the homes.

Though the dwellings seem vacant and safe enough, something about them doesn't feel right to him, so he moves on, knowing there are a few other houses up the road.

He's not sure why exactly he didn't enter any of the houses grouped together, but he trusts his instincts—and had long before this long dark ordeal began.

Since everything is open anyway, he walks the road, scanning the area around him, glancing over his shoulder often, always with his finger on the trigger of the 9mm in his right side duffel.

Up ahead he sees a small wooden farmhouse close to the road and decides to give it a try.

Before even approaching the house, he hides in the hedge and watches it and the area around it for a while.

He then walks around the yard, scanning the entire property and the forest that borders it and the area beneath the house.

Eventually, he steps up onto the small porch, stands to the side of the door, and knocks on it.

No one answers and no movement comes from inside.

He tries the handle.

It's locked.

He knocks again, then when there's still no answer, he kicks the old door near the handle and it pitches open, hitting the wall behind it hard.

The smell of death rushes out.

He swallows hard against his gag reflex.

Still standing to the side, he waits, searching the dark house from the cover of the doorjamb.

He can see very little.

Leaving the door open, he steps around to the back of the house and kicks that door in too.

And waits.

Eventually, he slowly, carefully enters the back door into the kitchen.

The bandana around his mouth and nose help, but the stench of death is still immense.

The kitchen looks to be untouched.

He quickly goes through the drawers and cabinets

closest to him, tossing cans and bottles and a can opener into his duffel.

You can sort it later. Just grab it and get out.

Only a few more cabinets to search through in the small kitchen.

Leave them. You've got enough. Get out.

Ignoring the voice in his head, he opens the remaining cabinets and drawers, rifling through their contents quickly, feeling guilty for taking things that belong to others—or once did.

He finds a couple of batteries, some wipes, a gallon of water, and some zip ties.

Okay. Time to go.

He starts to leave, but then hears something from another part of the house.

Death has been here, but what if life is still here too? What if he has just taken what still belongs to someone?

He pulls the handgun all the way out of the bag, and with it in one hand and his flashlight in the other, begins to move farther into the house.

—Anyone in here? he calls.

No answer. And no other sounds.

—I mean you no harm, but I'm armed. I don't want to accidentally hurt you. Please answer me. Is anyone here?

Still no response.

He moves into the small living room.

An old couch and recliner sit beneath dusty, bunched, and gathered slip covers, stacks of newspapers and magazines on the floor next to them. Small, rickety wooden shelves hold porcelain figurines and collectable plates.

A short hallway with three doors leads off the living room.

The center is a small bathroom with a pedestal sink, low commode, and a claw-foot tub with a handheld shower sprayer.

God what he'd give for a hot shower right now.

The door to the right leads to a cluttered catchall

room with a sewing machine, ironing board, and piles of clothes that smell of must and mothballs.

He approaches the third door.

He has saved this door for last because of how strong the smell of death is behind it.

The Skynyrd song echoes through his mind, leaving him with a nostalgic longing.

How many times had he heard it and in how many settings? While driving too fast. Class reunions. Throwing darts at the bar. Randomly on the radio. Blasting through the speakers of his crappy sound system at home.

Ooh that smell. Can't you smell that smell? The smell of death surrounds you.

With his back to the hallway wall, he opens the final door, his light and gun up.

Remaining in the hall, he scans the room, his eyes following the weakening beam of the light.

Need to recharge.

A small, sad dresser and chest of drawers, an old wardrobe, a nightstand with a Bible and a glass of water on it, and a small lumpy bed with a lifeless old lady on it, her body amazingly well preserved.

Not well preserved. Recently deceased.

Makes more sense.

No violence. No suspicious circumstances. Just quiet, peaceful death.

She had survived the end only to come to her own end a little while on. If it had only happened a few months before, she might have missed all the misery and malevolence that had been visited on the world.

He backs out and closes the door behind him.

He's about to leave when a thought occurs to him.

An old rural farmhouse like this wouldn't be on city water, but a well system with a pump. The pump wouldn't work with the power off, of course, but the hot water heater tank may still be full. If it is, he can take a bath. A cold bath, sure, but a bath.

He feels so grimy and oily, so sweaty and waxy that a

bath—even a cold one—sounds life altering.

It's too dangerous. Too frivolous for the world as it's presently constituted.

He can at least check. See if it's even an option.

Yes I can. I certainly can.

He steps into the small bathroom, looks around it one more time to make sure he hasn't missed anything, then turns the knob with the frilly cursive *H* on it.

The pipe spits and sputters and out comes clay-colored water with bits of dirt and rust in it that quickly washes away to run clear.

It's an option.

Worth it?

No, but I'm gonna do it anyway.

He quickly closes and locks the door.

Then, still holding the gun, he sets the light facing up on the toilet tank, places his bags on the floor, and undresses.

The small room is cold and he finds his shrinkage amusing.

It's about to get a hell of a lot worse, buddy.

He locates the soap and shampoo and turns on the water.

Gun in one hand, shower sprayer in the other, he sits in the tub and hoses his thin, pale body off with the freezing water.

It's as invigorating as it is cold and he begins to feel better immediately.

He can take the hunger and weakness, the fatigue and sleep deprivation much better than he can take having to go without bathing.

The soap makes his skin feel new again, and the shampoo makes his scalp tingle, his dirty, matted, in-desperate-need-of-being-cut hair feel as though it belongs to him again—and makes him feel human again.

From somewhere in the house he hears movement again. Or thinks he does.

He turns off the water and listens.

Nothing.

Pointing the gun toward the door and holding it there, he turns the water back on and finishes rinsing, his entire body tense and shaking.

Reaching a shivering hand up to turn the water off and return the sprayer to its cradle above the faucet, he recalls his night ritual of getting in Dawn's hot tub with her, their naked bodies enjoying one another and the Jacuzzi jets.

It's a thought that is both cruelly cold and warming somehow.

He gets out shaking and shivering, his teeth chattering, and towels off, listening for any other sounds, still holding the gun.

It's truly a shame to put back on his filthy clothes, but he has no choice.

He does, however, have clean underwear and socks—something to be truly thankful for. They're his last ones. He needs to wash everything soon.

As he's getting dressed, he continues to listen for sounds from the other side of the bathroom door, but hears none.

Once he is dressed, he swipes one of the LifeStraws from the bottom of his backpack, kneels down beside the tub, lowers the blue cylindrical filter into the dirty bath water, and begins to drink.

It always takes a few seconds of sucking before the cleaned water comes through the straw into his mouth, but when it does it is pure and refreshing and he always drinks far more than he needs.

He drinks and drinks and drinks, his other hand holding the gun up toward the door. By filtering and drinking the bath water, he saves the bottled water he has for those times when it is all he has.

When he can't take in another drop, he stands, his belly bloated and protruding out a little from his quickly diminishing frame.

He withdraws a fresh bandana from his bag, then

pauses. Is it time for one of the gas masks yet?

He decides to go with the bandana for a little longer.

Once he again has the backpack strapped on and the duffels dangling from his shoulders, he holds up both the light and the gun and prepares to leave.

He unlocks and opens the door, standing to the side and shining his weakening beam into the dim little house.

The light finds only empty walls and framed photographs.

He waits.

Nothing. No sounds. No movement.

Once he has seen all he can of the small hallway and the entryway of the living room beyond, he clicks off the light, then steps to the other side of the door and out into the hallway.

And waits.

Eventually, he clicks on the light and searches the living room with it.

Again there is nothing.

Beside him, out of the periphery of his vision, he can see that the door to the dead old lady's room is slightly ajar.

Thought I closed that.

You did.

Did opening and closing the bathroom door dislodge it?

Or is someone in the house with you?

Time to go.

The barrel of the gun follows the beam of light as it bounces through the living room and into the kitchen. He follows both, the excessive water he drank sloshing around his guts.

He stops abruptly as he sees what's on the small kitchen table.

Every hair on his body stands up, their follicles tingling as his blood turns to ice in his veins and he shudders involuntarily.

He really had heard something.

Someone has been in the house with him. May still be.

He spins around to check behind him, sweeping the light and the gun sight across the room.

No one is there.

He turns and looks out the back door.

Then around the room again.

When he still sees no one, he positions himself so that his back is to a wall, and looks down at the small, scarred table.

.308 Winchester. 150 grain. Full metal jacket. There in the center of it, is a single bullet and a single sheet of paper with a single line on it. Precisely printed in black ink.

What happened to the old man and the dog?

Fuck!

Somebody's watching him. Why? Following him. For how long?

The bullet is for a long-range high-powered rifle. Has he been in a sniper's sights? Is he now?

Pulse so thick in his throat he can't swallow and is having a hard time breathing.

Heart banging so hard, his entire body trembles with the bass drum boom of it.

Scanning the kitchen again, looking out into the living room, he wonders what to do.

Who the hell left this—

Doesn't matter. Just get out of here. Be careful, but get out. Now.

He's not sure why, but he grabs the bullet and piece of paper and shoves them in his pocket.

Kneeling, he unzips one of his duffels and pulls out the shotgun. When he stands again, he slips the 9mm into his waistband and prepares to leave.

Is he out there now? Waiting? Watching? Is he going to switch my lights off the moment I step through the door?

Or is he still inside? About to attack?

The type of bullet would seem to suggest that he's outside and will do what he will do from a distance.

I can't just run outside.

Think.

He grabs one of the kitchen chairs and slings it out the back door. It lands about ten feet out in the backyard.

Nothing happens.

He does it again. Throwing this one even farther.

Still nothing happens.

He grabs another, carries it with him as he carefully makes his way through the small, dark house. When he's certain no one is in the living room, he opens the front door and tosses the chair out into the front yard.

He then moves to the bathroom again, back to the wall, scanning the house with his light as he does.

Inside the bathroom, he closes and locks the door.

He then opens the window and looks outside.

It's only twenty feet to the woods.

It's your best chance. Go. Now.

He quickly scans the area, searching both the yard, the little piece of the road he can see, and the fringe of the forest.

Stepping on the toilet lid, he pushes up and crawls through the window. Coming down on the outside, his back foot catches on the ledge of the windowsill and he trips, falling down, his bags around him, hitting the ground hard.

Rolling.

The moment his body hits the grass, he rolls.

As soon as can, he pushes up—or tries to. He stumbles and trips and falls down again. The duffel bags keep him off balance as he tries to rise and run again.

Maybe someone is seeing him. Maybe not. But he's embarrassed by his spastic movements.

When he is finally able to stay on his feet, he begins to weave and zigzag to try to make a more difficult target, something that makes him feel infinitely silly, but something he does nonetheless.

Eventually, he makes it to the woods and begins using the trees for cover, bobbing and weaving between them, wondering all the while if he's being watched through a high-powered rifle scope.

6

From a distance.

Seen through a Bushnell Drop Zone scope.

Small, white painted wooden house.

A little over fifty yards away.

The old, modest home sits close to the highway—very little yard in front or on either side. More in the back. But not much more.

The four dots beneath the intersection of the cross-hairs moves from door to window to yard to hedge.

He's set up at an angle in order to see both the front and back doors. This leaves the far side of the house mostly hidden, but there is no perfect position.

Trees and plants block some of the front and near side too, but there are only two doors and he can see both.

The man had left the back door open when he entered the house through it. He had done the same, leaving it open when he left too.

His guess is if the man gets his message, he'll assume he's set up in the backyard and will run out the front. Of course, he could think that's what he's thinking and do the opposite.

Still can't believe he stopped for a bath.

Movement.

He sweeps the scope along the side of the house to the backyard where a kitchen chair has just landed.

Then another.

Is he seeing if I'll shoot? What a moron.

He starts to hit one of the chairs just to fuck with him, but resists the urge.

The front door then opens and he slings another kitchen chair into the front yard.

The fuck's he doin'?

He's tempted to shoot the chair, but again resists.

Only one chair left.

He waits, assuming it will be tossed into the front yard for symmetry sake.

But no chair is forthcoming.

He waits for a long while.

It bothers him that the bather didn't toss out all four chairs. He could see only doing two—one in each yard—but not three, not two in one yard and one in the other.

The house is perfectly still and quiet.

The fuck's he doin' in there?

Frozen in fear is a pretty safe bet. Or maybe he put his back out trying to throw the couch out the front door.

This brings a smile to his face.

Going in to get him is not nearly as fun, but at some point he's gonna tire of sitting here waiting while nothing is happening. And that point is nearly here.

7

Frightened. Moving fast.

He pushes through the trees, branches and bushes and undergrowth pushing back.

Drifting toward the edge of the woods closest to the road, he moves awkwardly, abruptly changing direction, bobbing and weaving his head like a boxer, attempting to make a difficult target to hit.

Zigzagging.

The Zapruder film plays on the movie screen of his mind.

Frame by frame. In slow motion.

26 seconds. 486 frames.

Street lined with people. Motorcade. Slow, stately speed. Black open-top Lincoln Continental limousine. Jackie's soft pink hat and jacket and skirt suit.

JFK clutching his throat with both hands. Jackie reaching for his arm with her white-gloved hands.

One moment later. An instant. A second. A few frames.

And then frame 313—the frame that gave Zapruder and a nation nightmares. Replaying over and over.

Kennedy's head exploding.

Rewind. Replay.

Kennedy's head exploding.

Rewind. Replay.

Kennedy's head exploding.

Rewind Replay.

Kennedy's head exploding.

Now, not Kennedy's, but his own. Whoever left the bullet and note, following him, tracking him, hunting him. His head seen through the crosshairs of a scope the way Kennedy's had been.

Explosion. Blood and brain splatter. Blast. Echo.

Stop it. Now. You've got to get it together.

He realizes how lax he's become in managing his thoughts, how mentally and spiritually lazy.

Keep moving. Make a difficult target. But quit obsessing. Stop imagining. Put a halt to all the rewinding and replaying, switching and superimposing. If you don't, you're going to drive yourself crazy.

He knows what to do, knows how to calm himself down and get his head right. But knowing and doing are not the same. Not the same thing at all.

Fear is no way to live—not even in a world like this one. Not even when there are legitimate things to be afraid of.

His biggest fear is not making it to help his family.

Can't help them if you're dead.

Can't help them if they're dead either.

Come on. That's not relevant to right now.

Breathe. Slowly. In and out. Three deep breaths. Concentrate on your breathing. In and out. Nothing else.

Stop feeding your fear. Thoughts will come. Nothing to be done for that, but let them go. Don't invite them to stay. Don't encourage them. Don't give them the keys. Don't let them drive. Just send them on their way.

He thinks about how he hasn't been praying—not

even for his or his family's safety. Why is that?

For a long time now, perhaps even most of his adult life, prayer had been listening, not talking. Doing, not asking. Prayer for him was action—creating, assisting, helping, extending himself for someone else. Prayer was connection—meditation, contemplation, reading, listening.

That's what it was. What is it now?

He hasn't been doing much of anything—only reacting, only responding.

It's as if he's shut down his spiritual side. Why?

What's the point?

Has what has happened caused him to stop praying, stop meditating, stop listening?

He has abandoned the very things that add so much value to his life, at the very time when the quality of life on the planet has plunged so low.

Is it because he's in survival mode, or something else? Anger? Disillusionment? Futility? Doubt? Grief? Numbness?

The question from a moment ago echoes through his mind again. What's the point?

The point is peace—the serenity and sense of wellbeing it produces, right? If so, the condition of the God-forsaken world, the absence of beauty or any sign of divinity, has nothing to do with it.

He's calmer now and doesn't want to think about it anymore.

He comes to other yards, a few random places where a lot or an acre has been carved out of the forest. Avoiding the open vulnerability of the lawns, he goes around them, deeper in the woods along the backside of the properties.

Eventually there are no more homes and yards, only woods, only pines and oaks and magnolias and birches and all the grass and weeds and kudzu growing between them.

He considers circling back to see if he's being followed, but knows he really doesn't have the requisite skills for something like that and would most likely waste a lot of time or get himself killed.

If he's being watched, hunted even, what can he do beyond what he's already doing?

In the late afternoon he pauses and prays for his and his family's and friends' safety.

8

Graying.

The landscape changes again.

As if fading into the muted palette of winter, the color drains out of the trees above and the brush below.

Everything is on the spectrum between black and white—wool, smoke, gunmetal, slate.

Pale. Pallid. Pasty.

Dull. Dreary. Dismal.

Soot on the ground. Ash in the air.

Pulling his bandana back up over his mouth and nose and his goggles down over his eyes, he continues through the charred forest.

Dehydrated. Wracked with hunger pangs. Exhausted.

Unable to go any farther without some water, a bite of food, and a bit of rest, he searches for a safe place to pause for a few moments.

He finds a ridgeline running perpendicular to the road and ducks down between it and the broad base of a large live oak tree.

Keeping his weapon at the ready, he removes a bottle of water from his left side duffel and begins to drink, reminding himself to consume it slowly lest it all come back up.

As he rehydrates, he scans the area around him.

No movement. No man or rifle.

He gives the water a moment to settle in his cavernous stomach, then goes back into his bag for a can of food and a can opener.

The cheap, shiny silver can opener has MADE IN CHINA stamped on the outside surface of the flat handle.

Seeing it makes him wonder how things are over there and in other parts of the world. Similar? Same? Worse?

Hell, he can't know for sure how they are in other parts of this country, let alone other countries and continents.

He looks at the can.

Van Camp's Pork and Beans.

420 calories. Cholesterol free. High in fiber. 98% fat free.

The can and can opener make metallic fumbling noises as he attempts to open it while holding the shotgun and watching the area around him.

He has never liked pork and beans, but when he has the lid off, he turns the can up and drinks them down like they're good, which in a very real way they are.

He thinks about how much of his previous eating was for pleasure as much as anything else. How often he had shared meals with family and friends, meals that were nothing short of celebrations of life and love, the mouths they used in engaging, interesting conversation tingling with the rich tastes of the flavors they loved.

He recalls chicken red curry from Thai Chef, sausage pizza from Pizzeria Napoli, the low country crawfish boils Dawn did for them in their home. Dear friends gathering to drink and dine and share life. Lynn. Dave. Aaron. Dan. Lou. Herbie. Non-Slutty Stacy. Sometimes Freda and Suz,

Peach and Slutty Stacy.

He had known how good they had it back then, had savored every second—something he's truly grateful for now. It hadn't taken losing it for him to truly appreciate it.

Will he ever have anything like that again? Is there the possibility of pleasure in the burned-out and brutal new world?

9

As he stands and begins to lift his bags back on, he sets the empty Van Camp's can on the ridge, wondering what he should do with it.

It's the same question he asks himself every time he eats.

The idea of leaving trash behind bothers him. He finds littering abhorrent. But it's not as if he can carry all his trash with him—and where would he carry it anyway? It's not like there are any open landfills anymore. The world is a landfill now.

How do you handle trash when the entire earth is trashed?

He can't convince himself that it doesn't matter. If anything, it matters more now.

He decides to carry the can with him, depositing it into the next trash pile he encounters, but as he's reaching for it, it explodes beneath his hand.

A moment later he hears the report of the rifle.

10

Nice shot.

The sniper had found his mark—from a fair distance and with a lot trees and smoke to contend with.

He'd been aiming for the red can but would've been okay with taking off the hand reaching for it.

Fucker had made a fool of him. He'd sat for over an hour watching the front and back doors of an empty house.

He's gonna maim him for that. See how well he does without a foot or a hand or with half his calf blown off.

He'll get to that—all of that all in good time—but first some fear and dread, fluster and panic.

11

Running.

Stumbling.

Duffels swinging from side to side, keeping him off balance, ricocheting him from tree to tree like a bumper pool ball.

Why the hell is he doing this?

Don't you waste a single second on why. There is no why—none you could understand. It's a complete waste of time and mental energy—energy you need to survive this.

He could've taken you out if he had wanted to. He's toying with you. Predator playing with his prey.

He had thought he was being hunted for food, but the note and can made it seem far more like sport. The hunter may have every intention of eating him, but he's clearly not starving and plans to play with him first. Of course, he could have no designs on dining on him. Could all be for fun.

Of all the things he gathered in the Army Navy and

Outdoor stores, a Kevlar vest and helmet never crossed his mind.

Coughing.

Hacking.

Gasping.

Soot and ash and smoke.

Difficult to breathe.

He's up by the road again. Close enough to see between the trees.

A forty-foot sailboat sits in the middle of the road, its ripped and shredded sails rippling in the hazy breeze, its rigging clanging rhythmically.

All the ducking and zigzagging, bobbing and weaving is exhausting, causing him to expend far more energy than he usually does during this same activity.

Up ahead in the road, a bridge extends across a stream, an overturned fire engine blocking all of one lane and some of the other.

The stream is higher than normal, the bridge his only option for crossing.

I'll be more exposed, but I don't have a choice, and I can use the firetruck for cover.

He pauses for a moment to consider it.

There aren't any other options, are there?

You could try to swim it.

And get everything wet, risk that the water is contaminated, and be an easy, slow-moving target.

You could walk along the stream. See if there's a better place to cross *farther down*.

Downstream will only get wider. Not to mention more treacherous. And get you off course.

So the road. The bridge.

Okay. Here goes . . .

I don't care how much of an idiot you feel like, zigzag like an alligator is after you.

Darting out of the woods onto the road, he dashes toward the bridge, moving from side to side, twisting, turning, jerking.

Frame 313 of Zapruder. JFK's head exploding, blood mist and brain and skull fragments flying into the air, his body slumping back and to the left, coming to rest in his wife's lap.

He thinks of the Van Camp's can and pictures the same thing happening to his head.

JFK clutching his throat. Jackie reaching for him. A moment later. An instant. A split second. A few frames. Kennedy's head exploding.

Faster!

Quit thinking and run! RUN!

He's running all out now, fast as he can with the weight and bulk of the bags he's carrying.

On the bridge.

Zigzagging. Twisting. Turning.

Ten feet.

No shots. Yet.

Ducking. Spinning.

Turn sideways.

Keep moving.

Overturned fire engine. Empty cab.

Seen at a glance. Not slowing. Not pausing. If anything, running faster now.

When you get to the back of the truck, pivot so that you're running in line with it. Let it block your body from view, from the shooter.

Falling.

Hard.

Hitting ground.

Pavement. Abrasions. Hide scraped off hands, knees, shoulder.

Am I hit? What happened?

Rolling. Turning.

As he rotates around, he sees the cable stretched across the bridge and the man who put it there.

He comes from the back of the firetruck, shotgun raised, pale skin pierced and inked with a plethora of Aryan and Confederate images and sayings. Late teens or early twenties. Shaved head. Pierced nose and nipples.

—What's in the bags?

—I have some food and water I can share. Here, I'll show you. Just put the gun down and—

He begins reaching into the bag.

—Stop right there or I'll blow your face out the back of your head. Now, are those there bags worth dying over? 'Cause if they are, I'll shoot you between the eyes right now, but if they ain't, I'd rather save my ammo. Don't have much left.

—Take it easy, Michael says, bringing his hand out of the bag and raising it along with his other.

—You can leave the bags and walk away. Just slip them off and walk out of here with your life. Simple as that. Or—

—No need for *or*, Michael says. I'll leave them and just walk away. I'd rather live than—

Split open. Spray of blood.

Eerily similar to what he had been remembering and imagining of the Zapruder film, the right side of the young man's head explodes. An open flap of skin and skull and hair hangs down as he slumps over toward and then onto the ground.

Michael scurries over to the back of the fire engine, his heart trying to pound its way out of his chest.

Pushing himself up, he tries to pull himself together as he estimates the distance to the woods on the far side of the bridge and how much of that span he would be protected by the firetruck.

Thirty yards to the end of the bridge. Another ten to be in the woods. If he sticks to the left side of the bridge and ducks into the woods on that side, he'll only be exposed for about ten to fifteen yards.

Go now.

He hesitates, scared, in shock from what he's just seen, from what lies just a few feet away in an expanding pool of blood on the pavement.

No better time than now. He's probably moving or

reloading. He'll expect you to be frozen in fear. Go. Now!

I don't want to die on a little bridge in the middle of nowhere so close to finally making it home.

THEN MOVE! NOW! RIGHT NOW, DAMMIT!

He does.

Head ducked. Shoulders hunched. Staying on a course that keeps him behind the firetruck. Zigzagging some. Dancing around like a drunk at an outdoor concert.

Twenty-five yards until the woods.

Please let me make it. Please let me see my wife and kids and parents again.

Fifteen.

Why the fuck is he doing this?

Why does it matter? He's doing it. Deal with it.

I am.

He's doing it because whatever kept him from doing it before is now gone.

Ten.

Five.

Woods.

As he stumbles into the woods on the left side of the highway, a magnolia branch near his head explodes, splintering the wood, fragments of leaves and bark raining down to the ground.

A moment later he hears the shot.

Dropping to the ground, he crawls for several yards—deeper into the scorched woods, farther away from the man firing at him.

Eventually, when the cover is thicker, he gets back up on his feet and begins to run again.

Still ducking and twisting and turning, but running. Running for his life. Running toward his life—toward those who had been his life and who were still.

12

How far will the sniper follow?

Did killing the man on the bridge satiate his appetite?

Is he still pursuing?

The actions and motivations of a man like him are impossible to predict—not with any certainty.

Before the old world ended, Michael had been a novelist specializing in crime fiction. He had studied crime and criminals, motives for murder, sociopaths, psychopaths, profiling, forensic psychology, yet it all remained a mystery to him—particularly the motives of madmen. The sniper stalking him now had interior motivations and fantasies fueling them he couldn't begin to understand, even if he were given access to them.

How far will the sniper follow—he thinks he may have his answer.

A burned-out pecan grove ahead serves as a gateway to a wasteland unlike any he's seen.

He approaches it slowly.

It's as if he's awakened on a distant, hostile, uninhabitable planet at the far edge of the solar system, marooned in a world man was never meant to be in.

It appears as though a hurricane has blown through, toppling tress and tearing up the terrain, followed by an enormous forest fire that somehow still burned every rain-soaked thing.

Damp dirt.

Scorched understory—brush and branches, grass and weeds, pine straw and pinecones.

Charred, soggy soil beneath his boots, thick gray haze swirling around him.

Smoke rises from the black earth like steam from a subway grate.

The quality of air is so poor here, the ground surface so impassible, the sniper would have to be suicidal to follow.

He reluctantly goes into his bag for one of the gas masks he carries. Not knowing how long they will last, he had wanted to wait until he was much closer to home to use them, but he has no choice.

Pulling the gas mask on, he adjusts the straps and secures it in place—a process made more difficult by his thick beard. He then withdraws one of the filters, removes the cap and plug, and screws it into the mask.

Slow down. Breathe normally.

It takes him a few moments to adjust to it, but when he does, the difference in breathing is incredible.

Keep moving. Duck. Turn. Zig. Zag. Use any cover you can. Even if the sniper doesn't follow you into this particular hell, he can still splatter your melon from far away.

He drifts back toward the road, needing to be close to the highway to keep his bearings.

Parts of the pavement are missing, huge chunks of the highway nowhere to be seen.

He remains as close to the road as he can, careful to use any cover available.

13

Something in the road.

Fifty yards ahead.

On a stretch of highway that appears largely un-scathed, a structure blocks the road, some sort of sign strapped to it.

There's a quality of light here he's never seen before. Between the low ceiling of smoke clouds and the scorched earth below them, an otherworldly yellow-and-orange glow permeates the planes.

And the light here is not the only eerie element.

There are no noises. No sound at all other than the ones he's making. His footfalls. His labored breathing inside the mask.

It's as if he's in an enclosure, a glowing, vacuous dome.

Adding another dimension of disquietude, all of this is experienced through the distancing and disorienting effects of the gas mask.

As he gets closer, he can see that the structure is a white cargo trailer with flat tires parked at a diagonal across the deserted highway—nothing else on the road for a mile or more in either direction.

Makeshift sign.

A painted piece of plywood tied to the side of the trailer with both nylon and grass ropes—the latter of which is singed and frayed—is one of the most disturbing sights he's seen since he's been on the road.

Yellow background. Black stripes around the edges.

WARNING spray painted in black above a crude but unsettling black skull and crossbones. Below it, also in black block letters: INFECTION.

In smaller print near the bottom: Danger. Keep out for your own safety. Turn back now. Nothing but death and disease beyond this point.

Beneath that, in the bottom right corner, a signature: Sheriff Raylan Caine.

You should turn back now.

No way. Absolutely not.

You're being a fool. Unnecessarily stubborn. Either they got out and they're alive somewhere or they didn't and they're dead. You're gonna do this for . . . what? What's the point? All you're doing is ensuring you'll never see them again if they got out.

He reaches into the right side duffel bag, turns on his audio player, and puts the earbud in his ear.

Hemingway's *The Sun Also Rises* begins where it left off the last time he listened.

Beyond the river rose the plateau of the town. All along the old walls and ramparts the people were standing.

Using the book to drown out the voices in his head, he walks around the trailer and continues down the empty road toward home, darkness descending around him.

14

Night fires.

Distant dots scatter across the black, barren landsa cape like a smattering of orange stars in a midnight sky.

Spray of arcing sparks.

Waves of slate smoke wafting through the woods, backlit by the burning black beyond them.

Hiss and sizzle and crackle.

Remnants of a recent burn in the pines. Black bark on long, barren bodies, small sections of fire still glowing near the tops like shimmering embers, sparks dancing in the glimmering waves and raining down to the smoldering earth beneath, bouncing on the blackened and charred ground.

Intense heat. Scalding. Stifling.

He's so tired, so utterly spent, it'd be difficult to walk under the best of circumstances. But here, in hell, he's finding it nearly impossible.

Smoke everywhere, thick as fog, impenetrable, unbreathable, unbearable.

Unable to do anything but slide his boots across the black pavement, he shuffles like the inmates in leg irons he used to work with when he was a prison chaplain—an occupation he did while learning to be a novelist, something that seemed now to be at least a couple of lifetimes ago.

Is it like this all the way to the coast or is there something different on the other side of this?

Shuffle. Shuffle. Slide. Slide.

No one can live in this. If this is all there is, there is no one left for him to find.

Told you this was a fool's errand. Turn back while you still can.

The filter canisters for the gas masks he has will last less then twenty-four hours—a lot less with the way he's been breathing.

Shuffle. Shuffle. Stumble. Stumble.

Not turning back. Can't.

Then you're a dead man walking.

Dead man shuffling. This brings a weary smile inside the mask.

He tries to focus on Hemingway's prose, but he's too exhausted, his mind too frayed, his body too hungry and thirsty.

Fires as far as the eye can see.

Low, flat land, trees thinned, missing. Spark and flame the only things visible in the blackness.

He feels as though he's in the desert, surrounded by the cooking fires of a million desert tribes. Nubians. Nomads. Natives.

Can't go any farther. Must stop. Must rest. Hydrate. Lie down.

Shuffle. Shuffle. Stumble. Fall.

He collapses, crumpling onto the hot, sooty pavement.

You should drink some water.

He knows he should, but he just wants to rest, to sleep, to not move a single muscle for a few minutes.

In another moment, he's asleep.

In his dream, he's John Jordan, the prison chaplain detective protagonist of a series of novels he wrote inspired by his experiences inside the big house.

Readers and interviewers had always asked how much of John is him. It had been a lot, but never all. Now, it is all. In the dream there is no separation between literary character and creator. He is John in a scene from one of the novels, questioning the morality of an action he's about to take.

Though he's standing in the middle of the compound of Potter Correctional Institution, a horn begins to honk.

Waking.

The horn isn't inside, but outside his dream.

Honk. Honk. Honk.

He opens his eyes to see headlights racing toward him.

Wearily, he pushes himself up off the pavement and slowly stands.

The moment is surreal.

He's groggy and fatigue-drunk, but even if he weren't, the moment would still be surreal.

Out of the smoky darkness, an ambulance, all its lights on—inside and out—speeds toward him.

Inside fully lit up. Brights on. Emergency lights flashing. Side lamps illuminating the blackness beside the road.

He's still dreaming. He has to be. There's no way a—

A siren pierces the silence.

He's awake and if he doesn't move he's going to be put back to sleep permanently.

He staggers to the edge of the road, but needn't have. The ambulance screeches to a halt just before it reaches him.

He can see that both the driver and the passenger have on yellow hazmat suits and self-contained breathing apparatuses.

There doesn't appear to be anyone in the back.

The driver rolls down his window about halfway, and Michael, placing his hand on the 9mm in his right side duffel, slowly approaches.

—What the hell are you doing out here? the driver asks, his voice muffled, barely perceptible.

He's a white man in his mid-fifties with extremely bright blue eyes.

—You're heading in the wrong direction, sugar, the fifty-something black woman in the passenger seat says.

—What're y'all doin' out here? Michael asks.

—Just made our final run. Thought we might save one more, but there's no one left.

—Where?

—We went as far as Clarksville.

—Poor souls, the woman says.

—I'm Lyle Doyle, by the way, the man says. This is my wife, Teesha.

—Michael, he says. Is it this bad all the way?

Teesha shakes her head.

—Clears up around 20, Lyle says. Gets fairly decent a few miles past 20 down 73, but not for long.

—Where you headed, sugar? the woman asks again.

—Wewa.

—*Wewa?* the man says. There is no Wewa anymore.

Even if his hometown truly doesn't exist any longer, he assumes this is the direction Meleah had headed when she left the canceled training in Marianna.

—What in the world for, honey? the woman says.

—Trying to find my family.

—Oh, she says. Bless your heart, baby, but there's nobody left.

—Y'all've been to Wewa? Michael says.

—Well, no, the man says. I'm tellin' you, you can't get to it. Roads are impassable. And even if you could . . . that close to the coast is underwater and or full of the infected.

He doesn't say anything, just tries to process what

he's heard.

—I'm so sorry, sugar, the woman says. But maybe they got out. Some did.

—What's your story? Michael asks.

—EMTs, Lyle says. Worked part-time for the ambulance service in Blountstown—back when there was a Blountstown. Been trying to do what we could to help since . . .

—Had the equipment and the knowhow, Teesha says. Be a sin not to help.

If any of his family and friends had survived and evacuated in this direction perhaps they had seen them. He reaches into his bag for his phone. The devise is useless except for the photos it contains—the only reason he has held onto it.

—Who you think you callin', sugar? Teesha says.

—I thought you may have seen or even helped some of my family or friends if they came through here.

—Might have at that, she says.

He depresses the button and waits but nothing happens.

It has been a few days since he's charged anything, and the phone is a very low priority compared to the flashlights and other survival essentials.

Unable to show them any pics, he describes several of his friends and family—including Dawn, Meleah, Micah, Travis, his parents Mike and Judi, and others.

—I'm not sure, Lyle says, but I don't think so.

—A couple are possibilities, Teesha says, but not for certain, you know?

—I believe my daughter was traveling this road. She looks a little like me.

They look at him more closely.

—Twenty-two years younger and a lot more beautiful, but . . . there are similarities. Her name's Meleah.

—Sorry, Teesha says, shaking her head. I don't think we have.

—You sure?

—Can't be certain, Lyle says, but we're pretty sure.

—Okay. Thanks. What happened to Blountstown? Michael asks.

—Flooded, Lyle says.

—Whole town underwater, Teesha adds.

—Hop in the back and we'll give you a ride, Lyle says.

Michael shakes his head.

—Thanks, he says, but I've got to get to Wewa, then Panama City, then Tallahassee.

—It's just not possible, friend. I wish it was.

—Got to try.

—Oh, honey, Teesha says. We understand, but . . . ain't no reason to get yourself killed too.

—What kind of infection is it? How bad?

—Deadly, Lyle says. It's . . . I've never seen anything like it. You can get it from the living or the dead. Seems like most of the dead have it. In the living . . . avoid anyone with bloodshot eyes and a reptile-looking rash on their neck.

—Where are y'all headed? Michael asks. Roads not passable in many places.

—A couple of miles this side of Marianna. We know how to get around the bad spots. There's a small area that's pretty much untouched. Sort of miraculous. A farm with a big barn set back off the road. We stay there with a handful of other survivors. We've turned a little country church nearby into a field hospital.

—We've saved a few poor souls, Teesha says. Come back with us. We can help you.

—Can't. Thank you, though.

—That's where we'll be, you change your mind. Come find us.

—Be careful up ahead, Michael says. There's a sniper. He killed a young white supremacist on a bridge not far from the area you're talking about.

They both nodded knowingly.

—Please change your mind and come back with us

now, Teesha says.

—I can't.

—Okay, Lyle says. We wish you luck.

—Don't suppose you have another one of those suits with you, Michael says.

Lyle hesitates.

—The truth is we do, he says. But I'll be honest with you, friend, I can't in good conscience let you have it. I hope you understand. I'm sorry, but if I thought you had any chance at all of making it, I'd let you have it in a heartbeat. But knowing what I know . . . it'd be like throwing it away—and we have very few left. I'm sorry, but . . .

—I understand. Thanks for being honest.

—Good luck to you, sugar, Teesha says.

—Y'all too, Michael says.

He steps back. The window raises and they pull away.

He begins walking toward Wewa as the flashing lights fade into the distant darkness.

He stumbles along, wondering if he's just made his biggest mistake so far.

What if you get yourself killed—a likelihood according to people who seem to know—and everyone's somewhere safe waiting for any word of you?

I just . . . I'm not sure what I should do, so I'm doing the only thing I know to do. I don't want to die, but I can't live without checking to see if any of them are still there. I can't.

He hasn't gone too far when the lights of the ambulance grow around him again.

Turning, he sees Lyle and Teesha heading back toward him.

What the . . .

He steps to the side of the road, removing the 9mm from his bag.

There's something about them that causes him to trust them for some reason, but he's been wrong before. Maybe they're coming back to try to take what he has or—

They pull up beside him.

Teesha rolls down her window.

—Whatcha got that out for? she asks.

—Habit. What're y'all doing back—

—Least we can do is take you as far as 20, she says. Get you out of all this smoke.

Tears sting his eyes.

—You sure? he asks.

—Put your gun up. Hop in the back. Stretch out. Rest. We'll have you to 20 and some breathable air in fifteen minutes or so.

—Thank you. Thank you so much.

He places the gun back in the bag but keeps his hand on it.

He climbs in the back and lies on the floor beside the gurney, not wanting to soil it with his sooty clothes.

Lyle and Teesha are likable and seem like genuinely fine people, but part of him can't help but wonder if this isn't what they say it is. Even if it's not particularly sinister. Even if they just plan to try to save him—drug him and take him back to their compound—believing that if he continues in the direction he's headed he'll be dead in less than a day.

Stay awake. Be vigilant.

He sits up and looks around. They are headed in the direction of Highway 20. Lyle driving, Teesha helping watch the road, neither of them paying him any attention, neither appearing to be up to anything other than what they told him they'd do.

They dim the lights in the back and, though he fights it hard, in moments he's fast asleep.

He wakes what seems like a minute later as the ambulance comes to a stop not far from the intersection of Highways 73 and 20.

He gets out, thanks them, and takes his mask off as he heads toward 20 and they turn around and race away behind him.

He hasn't walked far when he sees it.

The intersection of 73 and 20 is blocked by the convergence of some thirty or more abandoned cars.

His heart stops, stilling the ice cold blood in his veins as he sees that Meleah's car is among them, driver's door open, blood-covered airbag deployed.

**Part 3
The Deacon**

1

He races toward the car.

All previous weariness suddenly gone.

Glancing around, he realizes he's not being nearly as cautious as he has been, but simultaneously realizes he can't be. It's his little girl, his precious Meleah.

Is that her blood?

It has to be, right?

Her old Mustang is fire red with black interior. A love for Mustangs, like their love for smart suspense novels, horror movies, and romantic comedies, is something they share.

Reaching the car, he leans down and looks inside, the beam of his flashlight moving from blood-smeared airbag to seats, dashboard, floorboards, backseat.

There's no doubt it's her car—complete with extra pairs of shoes, old Starbucks coffee cups, and white hairs from her dog, Lila.

He misses her so much he wants to cry. And almost does.

Blinking back tears, he stands up and scans the area again.

All the vehicles around him are empty, most of them with their doors open.

Where are the bodies? Did everyone survive? Were the bodies moved?

Shutting off his light, he feels his way over ten feet or so, squats down and waits. It's too dark for him to see any movement, but he'd be able to hear it.

Nothing.

After a while, he snaps his light back on and begis moving through the vehicles again.

Looking. Scanning. Searching.

—Meleah, he whispers, even though he knows no matter what happened she wouldn't still be here. Meleah?

A few of the other vehicles have blood in them, some with deployed airbags, others with broken windshields, but no bodies, no signs of what happened to the drivers and passengers.

He searches the sides of the highway, the ditches and edges of the woods.

The area is largely clear and unscathed. There's a constant smoke-tinged north wind and he wonders if that has anything to do with it. Is it like an unseen Gulf Stream that keeps toxins and other harmful elements away?

It's so dark, so difficult to see, and his light has nearly lost all its charge.

It will be several hours before there's enough light for him to look around the entire area. Though he wants to look more now, he decides the best thing to do is find a safe place and sleep for a while.

He thinks about climbing into one of the vehicles and locking it—perhaps a van or extended cab truck, but realizes he'd be trapped if someone snuck up on him.

Wondering if the old roadside country store and gas station is still standing, he heads west on Highway 20 for a block or so to check it.

One side of the red, white, and blue awning over the

gas pumps is missing completely.

Gas nozzles on the ground, their black hoses coiled around them like snakes. Vehicles scattered around the parking lot and beneath the awning covering the pumps. Trash and newspaper boxes and random displays and supplies spilling out of the open doors of the only store for many, many country miles.

The two ice machines in front of the store sit open, empty, graffiti covered. THE END IS NEAR written on one. THE END IS HERE written on the other.

Be stupid to go inside.

If someone were inside, the doors wouldn't be open.

Withdrawing his 9mm from the bag, he slowly enters the open glass doors with it in one hand and his light in the other.

The cash register, its drawer open, is on its side on the countertop surrounded by a variety of products—from plastic soda bottles to packaged foods that should be rotting but are not because of all the chemicals inside them. Batteries, first aid items, hygiene products, fishing supplies, maps, all types of tape and tampons.

A cardboard cutout of a NASCAR driver drinking a Coke still stands not far from the huge blue fountain drink dispenser.

Mostly empty shelves running back toward mostly empty coolers—a few with their doors open.

A deli that once served pizza, fried chicken, and potato logs is empty, its carts and cookers overturned, its glass broken, graffiti on the side of its pizza oven.

From the bait box in the back, crickets chirp. They are the first insects he's heard in a month or more.

He searches the entire building—restrooms, storage room, office. No one is here.

Finding some string and empty cans, he ties a crude makeshift warning system across the front door opening, then leans against the back wall, his gun in his hand on the floor beside him, and falls asleep.

He's not sure how long he's slept when he wakes

with a start.

Someone's here. In the store.

He's unable to see or hear anything, but he senses someone. He has no doubt he's not alone.

What do I do? Turn on the light? Move? Wait?

He strains to hear any hint as to where the person is, but comes up with absolutely nothing.

Could it be an animal?

He's seen very few since the beginning of the end, but Jackson let him know there must be a few left somehow.

No, it's not an animal.

Slight? Why do I think the person is slight? Small in stature?

Maybe it's because we're all starving to death. He or she may *be* even skinnier than you are.

Maybe.

In the opposite corner of the store, diagonally from where he is, a small, faint penlight clicks on and begins moving around.

Whoever it is must not know I'm here.

As quietly as he can, he stands and begins to make his way toward the light. Leaving his bags behind, he takes only his flashlight and 9mm.

As he gets closer, in the tiny fraction of fill light spilling from the small beam, he sees a waifish teenage girl with jagged blond hair that looks like she hacked off herself.

She's attempting to get the last few drops from a green plastic two-liter bottle of Mountain Dew.

The clothes she's wearing, olive green tank top and a pair of wrinkled khakis, hang on her as if she's a cardboard cutout of a person instead of an actual living human being.

Something shiny, a necklace of some sort, hangs around her too-thin neck and dangles between where her cleavage would be if she had any, which she does not, and probably didn't before she began the starvation diet she's now on.

Coming up behind her, he clicks on his light and whispers to her.

—I'm not gonna hurt you.

She runs, but there is only wall.

—It's okay, he says. I'm one of the good guys. I'm not here to hurt you in any way.

She stands in a defensive position, ready to fight, ready to run.

Part of her hair is pink—a soft, faded pink that has mostly grown out now. Her left eyebrow is pierced. So are her ears—these last with several earrings rising up her entire earlobes. Beginning at the corner of her left eye and trickling down the side of her face are tattoo tears, but instead of green gang tears they are small upside-down pink hearts melting into tears.

He swings the light around on himself.

—It's okay, he says. You're safe. I'm not going to hurt you. I have a gun. If I wanted to hurt you, I could have already. I don't want to. See?

When he turns the light back on her, she's holding a large hunting knife in her right hand.

She's frightened, but she's feral too, and he wonders how long it has been since she's been around other people, wonders what all she's had to do to survive. How *has* she survived?

—I have some food and water to share. I truly mean you no harm.

She lets out a noise—something between a grunt and a growl.

—Let me get you some water. Sounds like you could use some.

She seems to consider it but doesn't say anything.

—I'm here trying to find my daughter. Her car is out there on the highway. I'd like to ask you some questions, but if you're too afraid to talk to me, I'll back away and let you go. It's up to you.

He begins to back away slowly.

—Wh . . . she begins breathlessly. Where . . . you . . .

come . . . from?

Her voice is not only small but her mouth and throat are dry, the sounds she's making alternating from airy to the parch-mouthed *smack* of skin sticking together.

—Atlanta. I'm from Wewa, but I was in Atlanta when all this started.

—Wh . . . What . . . is . . . it?

—What is what?

—This.

—An REM song, he says.

—A . . . Wh . . .

—It's the end of the world as we know it. But I don't feel fine.

—Wh . . . caused . . .

—Wasn't just one thing. I don't think. I don't really know.

—I . . . keep tryin' . . . to wake up.

He nods.

—Me too, he says. Worst nightmare ever.

—You're really not one of them?

—One of who?

—Them. The . . . Lefters.

—I don't know who that is. I'm not one of anyone except me.

—What's your daughter's name? What was she driving?

—Meleah. The dark red Mustang. There's blood on the airbag.

—They have her. She broke her nose when she wrecked.

—Who has her? he says, his pounding pulse pushing the rush of adrenaline through him. She's alive?

—Give me some water and some food and I'll tell you, she says. Try anything and I'll cut you up good.

He hears her but all he can think is She's alive. My Meleah is still alive.

2

—It's safest in the restroom, she says when they reach his bags and he's getting her water.

He hands her the small bottle.

—Drink it very slowly, he says. If it comes back up you'll be worse off than you are now.

She nods, but still drinks faster than he thinks she should.

—Why is that? he asks.

—Huh?

—Why is it safer in the restroom?

—There's a passage behind the paneling that leads outside. Can't get trapped.

—Then let's go in there.

She nods and begins to walk in that direction.

After he has lifted all his bags again, he follows.

—How long have you been out here on your own?

—Nearly the entire time. I guess I was with the Lefters about a week or so in the beginning, but been here ever since.

Her voice sounds better already, but he tries to keep her talking so she won't drink too fast.

—What's your name?

—I'm nobody. Who are you? Are you nobody too?

—I am, as a matter of fact, he says.

—Then there's a pair of us. Don't tell. They'd banish us you know.

—We've already been banished, he says. And there's no longer an admiring bog.

—Oh yeah there is. The Deacon is a frog with a thick fuckin' bog.

—The Deacon?

—The prick who has your daughter. He's the leader of the Lefters.

They walk into the bathroom and he turns on his light and closes and locks the door. She positions herself against the back wall and holds the knife out in front of her with both hands.

Placing his gun back in the bag, he withdraws a can of green beans and the can opener from the other bag and hands them to her.

She hesitates, but eventually takes them, keeping the knife in one hand as she does.

He sits across from her, his back against the thin, hollow wooden door.

With the knife in her right hand, she awkwardly opens the can.

—I understand you being cautious and think it's a good thing. I've seen some very bad things since all this began, but I'm as far away as I can be from you in this small room. I'm unarmed. And I'll hold my hands behind my head. Just don't hurt yourself with that knife and slow down. Don't eat so fast.

She seems to relax a little.

The small, dingy bathroom is dry as a bleached bone and long past smelling. The bare concrete floor is cool. Above the cracked porcelain sink with the pink highlighted blond hairs in it, an unframed mirror hangs on the wall—

something he's avoided so far.

—When you can, tell me what you know about what happened to Meleah.

—Let me finish eating and I'll tell you everything.

He nods and waits, looking more closely at the necklace dangling down from her neck. It's a simple chain with an antique-looking ring on it.

She's alive. Meleah is alive.

3

—The Deacon is a dangerous man, she says. So are the Brothers. Very. Nothing more dangerous than a self-righteous religious fanatic.

    —They part of a religious group?

    —They believe what happened was the Rapture and that we're now in the Great Tribulation.

    The Rapture and the Great Tribulation are part of Fundamentalist Christian eschatology based on a literal reading of the Bible. This type of Christian Millennialism is the result of misinterpreting and then cobbling together various passages from both the Hebrew Bible, particularly the Book of Daniel, and the Christian Scriptures, particularly the Book of Revelations. The simpletons and superstitious, the literalist and uneducated who subscribe to this form of Fundamentalist fairytale believe that Jesus will come down in the clouds and call his chosen to him—both living and dead—and that they will go back to heaven with him while a terrible time of tribulation will be unleashed upon the earth, after which time Jesus will return and reign as king for one thousand years.

    —So they actually believe they missed the Rapture, he says.

    Millennialism teaches that those left behind were not right with God—even if they thought they were—and are being given seven years in which to repent and get right with God before it's truly too late and they'll spend eternity in the torture of the lake of fire.

    —Yeah, for not being pure enough, not being strict enough, she says.

    —You called them Lefters, he says. Because they were left behind when the Rapture happened?

    —Uh huh.

    —Do they call themselves that or is that just something you—

    —They call themselves Disciples.

    He nods.

    —Deacon's got 'em convinced God has turned what the devil meant for bad into good, she says, that they are here for a purpose. They can miss the Great Tribulation if they will just follow the Deacon and do what he says. They're on a mission to be as pure as possible and to save as many others, making them as pure as possible too.

    —How?

    —Their discipleship program. The Deacon preaches all the time—is always getting new revelation revealed to him from God. He shares it and his gang of thugs, the Brothers, enforce it.

    —They use force?

    —When necessary. Mostly it's all done by manipulation. He's very persuasive. But yeah, the Brothers use force so the Deacon doesn't have to.

    —And they have Meleah?

    —They got everybody from the pileup. The Deacon actually hid the bodies of the ones who died in the wreck and told everyone the crash was caused by the Rapture, by some drivers being caught up out of their vehicles.

He recalls the oft cited passage from Thessalo-
nians. *Then we who are alive and remain will be caught up together
with them in the clouds to meet the Lord in the air, and so we shall
always be with the Lord.*

What's the other passage they use for the Rapture?
Oh yeah.

*As in the days before the flood they were eating and drinking
and marrying and giving into marriage until the day Noah entered
the ark . . . and the flood came and took them all away . . . so shall
the coming of the Son of man be. Then shall two be in the field . . .
the one shall be taken, and the other left. Two women shall be grind-
ing at the mill . . . the one shall be taken, and the other left.*

—His followers are just afraid, she's saying. It's
a scary fuckin' world. They're listening to the only man
around who says he has the answers—and he's so certain,
so sure, so convincing because of his conviction. And a lot
of his followers already believed some form of this type
of Fundamentalist end-time religion anyway. He just had
to convince them of their secret sin that kept them from
joining Jesus in the air. Which wasn't hard to do.

—No, I don't imagine it was.

—Can I have a little more water? she asks.

He finds some and gives it to her.

—You were part of this group? he asks.

—For a little while. I wasn't given a choice.

—How so? How do you know so much if you were
only part of it for such a short while?

—Because, she says, the creepy, charlatan cocksucker
running the whole thing is my stepdad.

4

Daylight.

Dew on the ground.

Compound.

He hasn't seen dew since this all started. Here, it's on everything—all the surfaces are slick with it.

Michael and Nobody are lying on the roof of the country store. Michael is studying the Lefters compound through binoculars. Nobody is beside him sketching with the nub of a No. 2 pencil in a composition book full of her artwork.

The Deacon had taken over Clarksville Baptist Church and its parsonage.

The small, white wooden country church is on a large lot—the entirety of which is surrounded by semi tractor-trailers. The trailers, many of them with the semis still attached at jackknifed angles, have been jammed in end to end, chain link welded to the inside to form a formidable fence.

The trucks and trailers all came from Shelton's Crossroads about ten miles or so up Highway 73, which gives them an evenness and uniformity that adds a certain aesthetic to the makeshift enclosure.

Inside the compound a network of RVs, campers, tents, storage containers, animal stalls, and gardens form a community centered around the small, white church.

Across the little road from the compound sits a small cemetery. Neglected now. Overgrown.

—My mom's buried there.

—Sorry, Michael says. Did she die before all this began or—

—During, she says, absently reaching up and touching the ring hanging from her neck.

—How'd it—

—Her heart was weak already, then the stress of all this shit, but mostly it was because that prick blamed her for him missing the rapture. Said she had never let him follow God like he knew he needed to, that she had always held him back. What she had done was serve him hand and fuckin' foot every moment they were together.

—I'm very sorry.

She doesn't respond.

—Was that her ring? he asks, nodding toward it.

She frowns and nods.

—It's all I have left of her.

—Why're you still here? Why haven't you moved on?

—To where? she says. Besides, the Deacon and I have unfinished business.

—What do you plan to do?

—Expose him.

—Can you wait until I get Meleah out safely before you do anything? he asks.

—Waited a while already. Little longer won't hurt.

He looks around the compound again.

—I can't figure out how to get in, he says. How'd you get out?

—Used to be a little gap in the fence in the back

right corner. They fixed it after I left. The only way in or out now is the front gate.

—Shit.

—I can tell you how to get in. It's easy. Getting your daughter and getting out . . . that's gonna be the hard part.

—How do I get in? he asks.

—You get rid of all your stuff, you lose the camo pants and boots, and you just start walking down the road. Let them find you. They'll invite you in and try to convert you.

He's about to say something when the front gate begins to open.

An armed escort walks a pale, chubby, blond-haired middle-aged man out of the gate and onto the road.

—That's two of the Brothers, Nobody says.

The Brothers were young militant-looking men with closely cropped hair and serious firepower. They wore black paramilitary-type uniforms decorated with random Christian iconography on them.

—So all she has to do is get banished, he says. If she hasn't already.

—She hasn't. I've been watching. No one has in weeks. But she won't anyway.

—Why's that?

—Look at the guy being banished. He's a fat, lazy lump of lard. Young pretty girls don't get banished.

The two thugs walk the excommunicated man down the road maybe a half mile or so as he pleads with them not to make him leave.

Coming to an abrupt stop, the Brothers pull their weapons off their shoulders and point them at the pale man.

It's obvious he doesn't want to, but he keeps walking. Slowly. Hesitantly. Continually looking over his shoulder. Begging. Pleading. Bargaining.

Eventually, the Brothers turn around and walk back to the compound and disappear inside.

—If he won't banish her, Michael says, I have to find

a way to get in and get her out. How many Brothers, are there?

—Too many for you to break her out. Think of something else.

He thinks of going back to the compound Lyle and Teesha mentioned to him for reinforcements. Maybe even to Marianna for Augustus. Be nice to have backup. Even a shooter up here in case things don't go as planned.

Be a lot better to sneak her out. Doesn't run the risk of her getting shot unintentionally.

—Will you draw a diagram of the compound for me? he asks. Label where everything is.

—No problem, she says, and immediately flips the page and starts on it.

—Would you be willing to help me? he asks.

—What am I doing now?

—With the escape. Would you be willing to create a diversion?

—I have grenades, she says.

—*Grenades?*

—Took them from the Lefters' arsenal. The Deacon had us using them on those things in the woods for a while, but there was just too many of them.

—Grenades will work great. Are you sure you can—

—I'm proficient as fuck with 'em. Won't hurt anyone I'm not supposed to—including myself.

—Let's don't hurt anyone. Let's just—

When Michael looks back up, he sees the chubby banished man jogging as best he can back toward the front gate of the compound.

—Look, Michael says. He's back.

Nobody looks up.

—Stupid motherfucker, she says softly, genuine pity in her voice. You don't get a second chance. He knows that.

—The Lord is my shepherd! he's yelling as he approaches. I shall not want! He makes me to lie down in green pastures! My cup runneth—

When he's within twenty feet of the front gate, his

head splits open not unlike the way Kennedy's had, not unlike the way Michael's would have if he hadn't eluded the sniper.

A spray of blood in the air above and behind him, the sound of the shot as he crumples in a sad fat heap on the asphalt.

Michael's stomach lurches and he feels like he's going to vomit.

The men who have Meleah are even worse than he realized. Far worse.

He begins praying for her. Sincerely. Naturally. Fervently.

So easy and automatic when it's for her.

The gate opens again and another pair of Brothers, this time in a small truck, come out. Wasting no time, they quickly lift and load the body into the back of the truck and speed away, driving around the pileup and heading east on Highway 20, disappearing from view in a matter of less than a minute.

—Let's start over, Michael says. Tell me everything you can about the Deacon, the Brothers, the Disciples, and the compound. Everything. No matter how small it may seem.

5

He is picked up on the road and taken into the compound and directly into the small sanctuary where a service is taking place and the Deacon is speaking.

It's evening. He and Nobody had spent the entire day making preparations for the breakout, including securing another semi tractor-trailer rig from Shelton's and hiding his stash of supplies and weapons in an old Ford pickup they plan to use in their escape.

Doing his best to appear docile, submissive, and a little lost, Michael sits quietly and listens intently, shrinking down into the pew as much as possible.

He mostly maintains eye contact with the Deacon but as he is able, he takes in the people and the place.

The Deacon is not what he had expected.

Young. Fit. Groomed. Bright-eyed. Well spoken. Clearly educated.

He's wearing a suit that appears tailor made, but only because of how well he wears it. His light brown hair is cut close and fixed simply. His mesmerizing blue eyes are both intense and empathetic.

—I believe we make this notion of repentance too complicated, he is saying. It's not complicated. It's simple. To repent means to change—change your mind, change your direction. You're thinking one thing. You realize it's wrong. You change your mind. You think something else. Simple. Not easy to do necessarily, but simple. You're heading in a certain direction. You realize it's wrong. You repent—you do an about-face and head in the opposite direction. It's that simple and difficult.

The sanctuary is small, simple, austere.

The Brothers are spread throughout—two on the platform with the Deacon, two at every exit, a few on the front row, some scattered throughout the congregation.

The congregation consists mostly of young women, but there are a few older men and some children smattered around. Not nearly as put-together as the Deacon, their appearance is far more mismatched and utilitarian.

And then he spots his beautiful brown-haired, brown-eyed girl.

She is sitting on the front pew on the left side, dressed in all white, her wavy brown hair cascading down delicately to rest on her dress.

Her eyes widen when she sees him. She glances at him, then away, but with a single expression and the quick, small shake of her head, she communicates for him to act as if he doesn't know her.

With the slightest of nods he lets her know he understands and with the briefest of expressions he reassures her everything's going to be okay.

—Perhaps before the Great and Terrible Day of the Lord we may have had time to repent, the Deacon is saying, may have had some leeway, but not now. Not when we're living when and how we are. Not when all around us there is death and disease and destruction. No. Now we must repent the moment—I mean the very instant—we receive the word from God. When God sends his correction now, we must heed it immediately. No delay. No discussion. No wavering, brothers and sisters. Just obedience.

This gets a reaction from the group. Lots of nods and a few *amens.*

—Let me remind you where we are, he says. Lest you forget, friend. We are part of the New Jerusalem. Set apart, consecrated to God. We are a holy people. A city set on a hill. We are the Land of Goshen. Just like God's people, the Hebrews, back in Egypt. Protected by the hand of God, by the blood of Jesus. Think of all that's befalling the world around us, but not us. Not us. We are blessed going in and blessed coming out. We are the chosen of God, a peculiar people. Priests and kings unto God Almighty. Do you doubt it?

The congregation doesn't doubt it and lets him know.

—Let me read something to you, he says, opening his large leather Bible. Listen to this. This is us, was written for us, about us, is true, prophetically, of us. See if it bears witness with your spirit.

He begins to read.

—*He that dwelleth in the secret place of the Most High shall abide under the shadow of the Almighty. I will say of the Lord, He is my refuge and my fortress: my God; in him will I trust. Surely he shall deliver thee from the snare of the fowler, and from the noisome pestilence. He shall cover thee with his feathers, and under his wings shalt thou trust: his truth shall be thy shield and buckler. Thou shalt not be afraid for the terror by night; nor for the arrow that flieth by day; Nor for the pestilence that walketh in darkness; nor for the destruction that wasteth at noonday. A thousand shall fall at thy side, and ten thousand at thy right hand; but it shall not come nigh thee. Only with thine eyes shalt thou behold and see the reward of the wicked.*

He places the Bible back on the podium, then walks about from behind it.

—Oh, friend. Please hear me. Please listen. *A thousand shall fall at thy side, and ten thousand at thy right hand; but it shall not come nigh thee.* If . . . *if* and *only* if we repent when God reveals our sin to us. Do you want to be part of us or part of the ten thousand falling beside us, all around us? Do you want to watch the reward of the wicked from the safe place here in the secret place of the Most High, here in the shadow of the Almighty, or do you want to *be* the wicked reaping the harsh reward, the destruction that secret sin brings down on your head?

They want to watch and not be the wicked and tell him so.

—Think about the world we now live in, the world that we are in but not of, he says. How true is the word of God? How accurate and precise when it speaks of the terror by night. You've heard the horror that comes from the woods at night. You've seen the abomination that now slinks its way across the earth. Think about it. What did the Psalmist call it? *The pestilence that walketh in darkness.* You've seen them or heard about them. You know what they're capable of. Do you want to be out there with them or in here with the righteous, the holy remnant of God remaining on the earth in these last days?

They definitely don't want to be out there with the pestilence that walketh in darkness, but in here with him, and they make sure he knows.

—Then, he says, when God speaks to me, don't just listen, really hear; and don't just hear, but perceive; and don't just perceive, but obey. Obey the word of God as it's revealed. Without question. Without hesitation. He who has ears, let him ear.

The congregation bursts into applause.

When they finish, the Deacon is looking directly at Michael.

—We have another lost soul in our fold tonight, he says. What's your name, friend?

—Michael.

—Stand up, Michael.

He does so very slowly, doing his best to seem timid and shy.

—Michael, like the archangel.

—Yes, sir.

—Sir? See that people? I'm younger than him, but he calls me *sir* as a sign of respect. He perceives the anointing of the Lord. Don't you, brother?

—I do, Michael says, nodding.

—Has the Lord God brought you to us, Michael?

—I have absolutely no doubt of that, he says.

—Did what I say—the Deacon begins, then corrects himself. Did what God say through me tonight bear witness with your soul, Michael?

—More than you'll ever know.

—Oh, I don't know about that. God reveals these things to me, brother.

Michael nods and bows his head slightly.

—I didn't mean that you—

—I know what you meant, brother. God knows. I know. Where do you come to us from, Michael?

—Atlanta.

—Atlanta? That's quite a ways away. Tell the people of God here tonight what you've seen out there, brother.

—I've seen . . . the terror by night and the pestilence that walketh in darkness.

This response makes the Deacon ecstatic, and following his lead, the congregation erupts with *amens* and applause and other affirmations.

Before becoming a novelist, Michael had been a theology student and a prison chaplain. He's familiar with people like the Deacon and their belief system, knows the language and how to use it, but will it sound sincere enough? Will he be convincing?

—So, Michael, the Deacon says when the crowd is quiet again. Where would you rather be? Here in the Land of Goshen or out there in the plague-ridden planet?

—Here. Here's where I want to be.

The congregation erupts again.

—And what will you do to stay here?

Michael begins to say exactly what he knows the Deacon wants him to, but figures that might be too suspicious, too much like a setup.

—Anything, he says instead.

—Anything, yeah, okay, but . . . brother . . . in the . . . on the backdrop of God's revelation to us tonight . . .

—I'll repent, Michael says. I'll hear the word of the Lord and obey without waiting, without questioning or doubting.

—Amen, the Deacon says. Brothers and sisters, I do believe God has brought us another new Disciple here tonight.

6

As Nobody had predicted, they put him in what they call the guest tent in the back corner of the compound.

The small tent is not only isolated, but located as far away from the front gate as you can get. If the guest tried anything not sanctioned by the Lefters, he or she would be spotted and stopped.

Because of the tent's position in the compound and its proximity to the back fence, Nobody had buried a couple of weapons beneath it before being banished. She was also right about it being a great place to toss things over the wall or pass small items beneath the trailer and between the chain link—such as notes and even weapons.

For tonight, he doesn't attempt any of those things. They have a plan in place and he plans to stick to it. Tonight he is only interested in being a docile, submissive Disciple, weary from the Tribulation going on outside the compound walls.

For tonight, he's just happy to be here—to have seen Meleah, to know she's still alive.

He knows he's being watched. And not only by the two Brothers guarding the gate. Thanks to Nobody, he knows most of what's going on around him—and where and who's involved. Unless it has changed since she was here, he knows who is in each RV and tent and what is in each storage container. She had told him where the bathroom and showers are—something that almost led to a fateful mistake when earlier in the evening he had started to walk over to them without asking anyone where they were. She'd even told him where the gardens are—though the crops have changed since she was here. She had also been right about the single gate serving as the only entrance and exit being as much a liability as an asset.

In addition to having two semi tractor-trailers full of nonperishable food the Brothers had gathered from a fifty-mile radius, they are growing their own food—including raising livestock for milk, eggs, and meat.

Michael's trying to figure out a way to get a little sleep without totally letting his guard down for any real length of time, when a shadow appears at the front of his tent.

—Brother Michael?

It's Meleah's voice.

—Yes, he says, scurrying over to unzip the tent. Come in, please.

—I can't come in, she says. It'd be improper and disrespectful to the Deacon, but if you could step out here for a minute . . .

—Oh, sure. Sorry.

She's just as beautiful, her big brown eyes just as intelligent and kind, but there's a weariness and wariness about her not there before. A sadness too.

His little girl. One of a small group of people on the planet he feels utterly responsible for. He's overwhelmed to see her, overcome with the desire to hug her, to grab her hand and run.

She is holding a basket, which she hands to him when he's out of his tent and standing before her.

—The Deacon and I would like to personally welcome you with this token of brotherhood and friendship.

He tries to read her eyes.

She nods and attempts to communicate something to him but he's not sure what it is.

She glances down at her hand and widens her eyes as she reaches out to shake his.

—Blessings be upon you, she says, shaking his hand as she brings her other one over to pat his other.

He's so happy to be so close to her, to actually be touching her again that it takes a moment or so for him to realize that there's a folded piece of paper in her small hand.

—We'll wake you for work in the morning, she says. Rest well. You're safe here. Good night and God bless.

As she turns to leave, he holds the note so that the basket conceals it.

—Night, he says, then watches her as she walks across the compound to her camper, which he can't help but notice is right next to the Deacon's parsonage.

Heart happy, he rushes back inside his tent, zips it up, drops the basket of hygiene products, Gideon Bible, paper and pencil, and begins to read the quickly scrawled note written in her own hurried hand.

I can't believe you're here. I'm so happy to see you. I never thought I would again. I wish you weren't here—these are very dangerous men—but I'm so glad you are. I'm okay. Actually, being treated like a queen. That's because the Deacon has designs on me. He hasn't tried anything yet, but I can tell it's coming. They've made it clear that I can't leave—though I didn't think I could survive for long outside anyway. Any word from Micah, Travis, Mom, Mema, Papa, Taylor? Are any of them alive too? Listen to me, Dad—leave while you can. They'll kill you if they find out who you are, and there's no way you can break me out of here. There are too many of the Brothers and they are too well armed. Most of them are sociopaths like the Deacon. I love you so much and just knowing you're alive means more to me than you'll ever know. Take care of yourself and the rest of the family. Now that I know you're out there—and maybe others too, I'll escape when I get my chance. Or if any kind of order is ever restored to the world, which I know is very doubtful from the look of things, send the authorities to shut this place down. I was always going to make a move before I was forced to become his bride, so . . . Love you. Destroy this letter as soon as you read it. They routinely search the living quarters for contraband. They'll kill us both if they find this.

He reads it three times, then rips it into strips and eats it.

She is so brave, so strong. Always has been. But she can't really think he'd leave her here, that he wouldn't risk everything, including his own life, to save her.

He thinks about what he should do. Will the plan work? Can he trust Nobody to carry it out? Should he go get help and come back? But who? Augustus? Lynn when his leg has healed? Lyle and Teesha's group? Continue to Wewa and see who's alive there who might help?

He doesn't want to wait, doesn't want her to be in this toxic place one more second, but he doesn't want to do something that will cause her to get hurt or killed.

Fuck!

He's just not sure what's best.

7

He falls asleep thinking about what a strong-willed and independent child Meleah had been. She had arrived with an extraordinary sense of self. She knew what she liked and what she wanted—and good luck talking her into anything but. Rarely would she accept help with anything she could do for herself, and she had a fierce determination to do most everything for herself. With dogged determination she set her steel-like will to learning to tie her shoes, read, ride a bike, dress herself, fix her own hair.

He smiles as he recalls the extended period of time prior to starting school that she not only wanted to dress in her Disney princess costumes every single day but insisted on being called by their names.

I'm not Meleah, she'd say with frustration and conviction. *I'm Ariel.*

Another day it was, *I'm not Meleah, I'm Jasmine.*

Still another day it was, *I'm not Meleah, I'm Belle.*

He had watched the old VHS tapes featuring the Disney princesses over and over and over and over again with her, wearing out the tapes and buying replacements.

He had always been completely involved in her life, but became her primary caregiver when she was three. He was a full-time student with a flexible work schedule who kept Meleah while her mom started a new career. Caring for her had been at the center of who he was, who he had always been, and it had been something he had done, in various ways and to varying degrees, her entire life.

He had seen taking care of her, protecting her, not only as his primary purpose but as the greatest privilege he'd ever been given. And he had felt the same way when her little brother Micah had arrived. And again later when Travis had joined the family.

Just before succumbing to sleep, he recalls how protective—some would say overprotective—he had always been over his kids. Believing it was his job to get them safely to adulthood, he had attempted to see accidents before they happened and prevent them from ever occurring—a skill he had perfected over the years, one that his wife, Dawn, who took a different approach with her son River, laughed at him about. But Meleah's only significant childhood injuries—slicing her tiny thumb open when reaching for a knife on the kitchen counter and burning her little arm while reaching for a cookie on a cookie sheet that had just been pulled from the oven—occurred when he wasn't around, when he was at work instead of working to prevent her from experiencing serious injury.

She's an adult now and for many years has needed him nearly not at all. But she needs his help now, and that part of him that wants to protect her from people like the Deacon and events like the apocalypse is still every bit as resident in his core as it ever was. Maybe more so.

8

Morning comes.

He's slept very little.

He's spent the night thinking about what he should do and still doesn't know.

All he knows for sure is if he's going to change the plan it has to soon. Otherwise, when noon arrives so will Nobody. The balloon will go up and it will be too late then to do anything but see the plan through.

But is that true? Can he really count on her to do all she's supposed to? It's a lot to ask of someone he barely knows. And she's not much more than a child. A damaged orphan with heart tear tattoos.

Yeah, I need to rethink this plan. It relies too heavily on her.

Everyone gathers in the sanctuary for morning prayers and he realizes what this all reminds him of. It's like one of the religious summer camps he went to in early adolescence. Or maybe more accurately it's like life in a monastery—religious duty and observation integrated into every aspect of daily living.

He is greeted warmly by the other members of the community, treated with kind regard by everyone he interacts with.

These are decent people. Why are they following someone like the Deacon? Why have so many millions and millions of well-meaning people trusted and followed monsters throughout human history?

Concerned someone will notice the family resemblance he shares with Meleah, he keeps his head down, letting his hair hang down over his face, grateful for his thick beard and disheveled appearance.

On the walk over to breakfast, he is joined by the Deacon and Meleah.

—What do you think of our little Land of Goshen? the Deacon asks.

—That's exactly what it is, he says. A haven. A sanctuary. Do you think there are others around the world?

The Deacon nods.

—God always has a remnant. God's people, the body of Christ, is present in every nation of the earth. Like us, they are people who had been deceived but now see the truth, who had been drinking and marrying and giving into marriage until Noah closed the door to the ark and the rains came and the flood carried them away.

Michael nods as if he not only understands but agrees.

—Not that there's anything wrong with marriage, the Deacon says, leering at Meleah lasciviously. It's an honorable estate given to us by God because it's better to marry than burn.

The thought of this sociopath burning with lust for his daughter is nearly too much for Michael and he has to change the subject.

—Do you ever send out search parties? he asks. Then realizing his mistake adds, I mean missionary parties to find others and share the message of repentance with them?

—We believe God brings those to us who are meant to be here. Like you, Brother Michael.

—Amen, Meleah says softly.

9

At breakfast, beneath a pavilion in the back left corner, with everyone gathered, the Deacon looks across the length of the table they're sitting at opposite ends of and locks eyes with Michael.

—So, Brother Michael . . .

Everyone stops talking and even eating and listens.

—Yes, sir?

—What secret sin was it that caused you to miss the Rapture?

—I've been thinking about that a lot since it happened—even more after your message last night.

—And?

—I believe my main sin was that of pride. I thought I was right with God, but well, it was a self-righteousness, based on my own merit and works. I don't know . . . I could be wrong, and I'm sure over time I will see more, but . . . I thought I was a good person and that that was enough.

The Deacon nods his approval as Michael speaks.

—Our righteousness is as filthy rags—literally menstrual pads—compared with the righteousness of God, the Deacon says.

Michael lowers his head even more and nods.

—I see now mine was, Michael says. Still is. But now I'm relying on the grace of God and the blood of Jesus.

—You say all the right things, the Deacon says, but . . .

Michael raises his head and locks eyes with the Deacon again.

—But? Michael says.

—I don't know. I just wonder . . . are you who you seem to be? Do you really mean what you're saying?

—A tree is known by its fruit, Michael says. Talk is cheap. Everything is made manifest in time. I can leave if you think that's best, or in time . . . who I am, who we all are, will be made clear.

—Yes, it will, brother. Yes it will. Stay. Work beside us and let God make everything plain.

10

He's been here such a short time and is already under suspicion.

I was afraid of that. I'm saying the right things—too right, I guess—but my lack of conviction is showing through.

Means he can't wait. He must carry out the plan at lunch today.

Going through everything over and over again as he helps around the compound, he prepares himself for what he's about to undertake, for what could cost him his or his daughter's life.

Can he do it? Can he really risk his little girl's life?

What choice do I have?

Is there any way to save her while also guaranteeing her safety?

Would she be better off if I do nothing? Would life here in this compound be better than no life at all?

Hasn't she already answered that? She said she was

going to make a move before being forced to be his bride.

During his short break before lunch, he cuts a hole in the back corner of the tent and removes the weapon buried there—a rusty and pitted snub-nose .38 Smith & Wesson with five rounds in it and a hunting knife.

Hiding them in the waistband of his jeans and making sure his untucked shirt covers them, he goes to lunch early to sit as close to the Deacon as possible.

11

—How can I be of the most service here? Michael asks.

The Deacon is at the head of the table. Michael is in the seat next to him, Meleah across from him in her usual place of honor.

—That will be revealed in time, brother. Be patient. God gives each of us gifts to use for his glory. Each of us is a different member of the body of Christ and each does a different task, performs a different duty. In time your place here will be made manifest, but I've got to tell you . . . I see great things here for you.

—I just want to serve, to do my part to—

—You will, the Deacon says. Excuse me a moment while I address the congregation.

He stands and begins to say a few words and quote a scripture in preparation for blessing the food.

Nobody said this would be the best time to attack because the entire group would be in one place at one time—with only one Brother guarding the gate where normally there are two. It's also the best time because with no clocks and effectively no time, using the midday lunch hour is the surest way to synchronize the plan.

—But before I do that, the Deacon is saying, I have something I need to do first, something I want all of you to be witness to. As you know, my wife was weak, a test sent to me from the Lord. I passed that test and the Lord took her when the Great Tribulation began. Since that time, I have been praying for God to send me a helpmate, someone who can serve me as I serve the Lord in this vital end-time ministry. Well, the Lord God has heard my prayers and brought to me a young woman who I know my soul can be knit to. Y'all know I'm talking about Meleah, and today, in front of all of you, our true family, I'm asking Meleah to marry me, to become my full partner in all of this, in all of life.

He doesn't get on one knee or really even address Meleah. He is their leader, the embodiment of God on the earth and he will not be seen bowing before anyone.

—I believe God is calling you to be my wife, he says, finally looking at her. Will you answer the call and be my bride, the bride of Christ?

There's a reason he's had her wearing all white and sitting on the left side of the sanctuary—the side the bride traditionally stands on during a wedding.

Meleah looks at Michael.

He nods and signals her with his eyes that shit's about to go down—though he has no idea what message she receives.

She slowly stands. Beautiful. Radiant. Clearly apprehensive.

Thankfully before she has to lie to stay alive, the Deacon's stepdaughter begins the diversionary tactics, the balloon goes up, and the plan to rescue his daughter is underway.

12

Gunfire.

Grenades exploding.
Molotov cocktails raining down around them.
Pandemonium.
Screaming.
Yelling.
Running.
People begin to climb to their feet, knocking over their chairs and the table as they do.

—We're under attack! one of the Brothers yells. Man your positions!

As members of the congregation run for cover, the Brothers draw their weapons and move toward the wall.

—Relax, brothers and sisters, the Deacon says. No weapon formed against us can prosper.

—Let us get you to safety, one of the Brothers says to the Deacon.

—Just respond to the enemies of the Lord at the

gate. God will protect me.

—Do you know who it is? Michael asks. Does this happen often?

—All enemies of God are the same, the Deacon says. Deceived and defeated.

—Everyone return to your living quarters, another one of the Brothers says. Await instructions there. We'll have this taken care of in no time.

As everybody scrambles, only the Deacon, Michael, and Meleah remain standing still.

—You're not frightened, are you, brother? the Deacon says to Michael.

—Like you said, no weapon formed against us can prosper. *He that dwells in the secret place of the Most High shall abide in the shadow of the Almighty.*

—Amen, brother. Amen. You're absolutely right. But for the sake of order and wisdom, let's return to our living quarters while the Brothers take care of this.

Michael nods and slowly turns and begins to walk toward his tent.

—Come with me to the parsonage, the Deacon says to Meleah. We can see what's going on outside in the monitors. We have cameras set up along the perimeter.

He takes Meleah by the arm and leads her toward his house, making a point to walk upright and slowly, showing no fear.

It doesn't take long for all the members of the congregation, mostly women and a few old men, to disappear into their living quarters. Only the Brothers remain visible on the compound, and not only are they distracted dealing with the fireworks, but the direction the Deacon, Meleah, and Michael are walking takes them farther and farther away from them.

As Michael nears his tent, he ducks behind a storage container and doubles back toward the Deacon and Meleah.

Please protect her. No matter what happens, please keep her safe and help me get her far, far away from here.

Nearing the parsonage now, the Deacon is walking faster, pulling Meleah along beside him.

Michael scans the area around them. No one is in the vicinity. Pulling the .38, he comes up behind the Deacon and presses the barrel to his temple.

The Deacon stops walking. Without moving his head, he cuts his eyes over toward Michael.

—You? he asks in surprise.

—Let go of her.

He does as he is told.

Meleah steps back beside her dad and he hands her the knife.

—You're behind all this? the Deacon says. For her? You're here for her? Who are you?

—I'm her father, you creepy motherfucker.

—Why do all this? Why not just leave? We've never held anyone against their will.

—Then help us escape quietly now.

—Sure, but why not just let me lead you out the front gate?

—Because I saw what happened to the last person who went out the front gate.

—What? What do you mean?

—He was gunned down in the street, killed for trying to get back in.

—No way. I would know if that—

—Walk, Michael says, pressing the gun even harder into his temple.

He wonders if it's possible the Deacon really is ignorant about what happened to the pale chubby man who dared to come back after being excommunicated, but decides there's no way he doesn't know everything that happens here.

I bet the order came from him.

—Where are we going? the Deacon asks.

—To the fence behind your house.

He continues walking in that direction without hesitation, seemingly unafraid.

—I meant what I said, the Deacon says. No weapon formed against me shall prosper.

—Just walk.

—Was everything you said a lie? he asks. All the scripture, all the . . . Are you a wolf in sheep's clothing?

—That would be you, Michael says. I'm more a sheep in wolf's clothing.

—But—

—No decent person seeks power over people the way you do. No sheep wants to control and enslave and rule and be worshiped.

Eventually the gunshots and explosions from the other side taper off and cease, and there is only the fire started by the Molotov cocktails.

A few moments later there's what sounds like a wreck near the front gate.

—What was that? the deacon asks.

—That was Nobody, Michael says.

—Huh? What was it?

—What it was supposed to be was another semi tractor-trailer from Shelton's blocking the front gate to discourage y'all from following us.

—We're not gonna follow y'all.

—Come on, Michael says. They'll be coming.

When they reach the fence, Nobody is there beneath the trailer cutting the chain link with bolt cutters.

When the Deacon sees her he shakes his head and laughs.

—Should've known, he says. Let me tell you something, Brother Michael, you've hitched your wagon to the wrong mule. Talk about a leaky bucket. You're in real trouble if you're counting on her.

—Don't say another word about her, Michael says. Don't even look at her. Don't look at either of them.

She finishes cutting the fence and pulls it to the side for Meleah to crawl through.

—All that talk about repenting, Michael says. Think about trying it yourself. The passages you use to make sense of what's happening were written about other things—mostly events that happened around 70 AD, but none of it, *none of it* was written about you or this place or what's happening now.

—Why don't you stay and let's discuss theology a while, the Deacon says. I'd really like that.

—Another time, Michael says. If our paths ever cross again.

—Oh I have no doubt they will, the Deacon says. No doubt.

—Until then, then.

—It didn't have to go this way, the Deacon says.

—You're right. Could've been much, much worse. Remember that when the duller side of you wants to retaliate. Also remember what your stepdaughter can tell your congregation about you. Now, sit down here and back up to the fence.

—I don't know what she told you, he says, but she's a sick little girl, as crazy as her mama—and that's sayin' something.

Michael gets on the ground and backs through the hole in the fence so he can keep the gun on the Deacon.

When he's out, he has the Deacon slide all the way back to the fence and put his hands behind him through two of the holes in the chain link. He then zip ties his hands at the wrists as Nobody twists wire around the loops she cut.

—Did you save one for me? Michael asks when she's finished.

—Yeah. Here.

She hands him a plastic shopping bag like the ones so ubiquitous before the end began.

—You're carrying them around *in a plastic bag?* he asks in shock.

—Why not?

He shakes his head.

—Head to the truck, he says. Get to a safe distance. I'll finish here and be right behind you.

—Dad? Meleah says, coming back toward them from a few feet into the woods. We need to go. Now.

—We are. Go with . . . her. I'll be right behind you.

—But—

—I'm coming. I promise. Go. I'll be right behind you.

She reluctantly goes with Nobody.

When they are gone, he withdraws the grenade from the plastic shopping bag and places it in the Deacon's hands.

—Don't let go, he says, and pulls the pin.

—What the . . .

—This is just to give us a head start. I sincerely hope you won't come after us, but I don't think you're smart enough not to. Eventually, y'all will get the front gate open and someone will come around here to remove this from your hands, but hopefully we'll be halfway to Marianna by then.

—We won't come after you, he says as if weary of saying it.

—You should know there's nothing I won't do to protect my daughter. You got off easy this time. If there's a next time, no matter what else happens, you won't. It won't go well for you.

—You know why we're not coming after you? the Deacon says.

Michael doesn't say anything.

—'Cause y'all won't last a day out there. You with two fragile young girls. Not a single day. You reap what you sow. You'll get yours. God'll see to that. *Touch not my anointed and do my prophets no harm.* You've sealed your own fate, friend.

—Are you a prophet or a confidence man who hid some bodies after a car wreck and cried Armageddon?

Michael stands to leave but turns as he sees movement out of the corner of his eye.

Nobody is coming up beside him, the small .38 he had earlier in her outstretched hand.

—What're you . . .

She doesn't stop until the barrel is pressed to the back of the Deacon's head.

—Don't, Michael says. You shoot him we're all dead.

—Your daughter's waiting for you in the truck. Go.

—No. Come with us.

—Go. Now. I'll make sure you're not followed.

—All you'll do is get yourself killed.

—I'm already dead. I've been infected. Only thing keeping me alive has been this—this moment.

She jams the barrel of the gun even harder into the back of his head.

—Tell Michael how many times you raped me. Tell him.

Now he understands the tear tattoos, the hacked off hair, the distrust and disillusionment, the distant stare.

—I . . . I didn't rape you. We're not related. Sins of the flesh are as nothing compared to the sins of the spirit.

—You need to go now, Nobody says to Michael. I wanted to wait until his little sheeple gather around so they'll know what a fuckin' monster they've been duped by, but don't think I'll be able to.

Michael falls to his knees and grabs the grenade, holding it tightly as he removes it from the Deacon's hands.

—What're you—

—You want to kill the monster, fine. It doesn't help like you think it will—but I understand. Just don't kill yourself too. Do what you have to and come with us. Now. Let's go.

She nods.

And pulls the trigger.

Nothing happens.

She fires again, and again nothing happens.

The Deacon begins to laugh.

She pulls the trigger again and again and again.

—I told you no weapon formed against me would prosper, didn't I? I told you.

The Deacon sounds surprised but elated.

—I told you. This proves it. I am a prophet of God. I am.

—Come on, Michael says to Nobody. When we're far enough away I'll toss the grenade back.

She shakes her head and removes the rusty hunting knife from beneath her shirt.

—Say it again, she says. Say it again.

—No weapon formed against m—

While he's speaking she slides the blade across his neck, slitting his throat open. Blood spurts out and he begins to cough and spit and sputter.

—Say it again, she says. Say it.

Michael grabs her arm and pulls her.

—Come on. We've got to go. Now. You did it. You silenced the false prophet. You slayed the dragon. He's dead. Let's go.

He drags her through the narrow path in the woods to the old pickup on the shoulder of the road where Meleah waits for them.

He jumps in the driver's seat and Meleah slides to the middle as Nobody climbs into the passenger seat.

As he puts the old truck in gear and it rattles away, Meleah grabs him and hugs him, giving him one of the tightest, most enthusiastic hugs she ever has.

—Thank you. Thank you. Thank you. I love you so much.

—I love you, sweet girl. Are you okay?

—I really am. I'm . . . I just feel so relieved.

He drives down the little side road until he reaches the intersection. Without stopping, pausing, looking, or even slowing, he turns onto Highway 73 and continues his journey toward home—this time with his daughter beside him.

In less than a mile, the climate has changed again—as has the environment.

In less than two miles, four armed Brothers on motorcycles are chasing them.

—*Shit.* I forgot they had motorcycles outside the

fence, Nobody says as bullets begin ricocheting around them, pinging off the tailgate and bumper, shattering the rear glass and side mirrors, and dashing their hopes for a quiet, smooth escape.

Part 4
Perish Twice

1

Racing down Highway 73.

Old Ford truck.

Motorcycles in pursuit.

Shots fired. Then others.

—Get down, Michael yells, reaching over and pushing the two girls' heads down as he ducks down himself.

This leaves the hand holding the grenade on the wheel—something he realizes only after he's done it.

Bullets begin ricocheting around them, pinging off the tailgate and bumper, shattering the rear glass and side mirrors.

Bringing his right hand back up to grab the wheel, Michael carefully removes his left, gripping the grenade with increasingly moist fingers.

—I'm such a fuckup, Nobody says. We're gonna die and it's my fault.

—Are you kidding? Meleah says. You're the reason we're out.

—We're not gonna die, Michael says. Meleah's right.

This is not your fault. Just stay down.

Bullets continue to buzz around them.

The four Brothers are in all black, including black helmets with black mirrored face shields that hide their identities.

Coming up fast. Two on each side of the truck.

After taken the grenade from the Deacon, he hadn't wanted to draw attention to their whereabouts by tossing it into the woods and letting it detonate, so he had brought it with them, planning to dispose of it once they were several miles away. But now it just might be the thing that saves their lives.

—Buckle up, he says.

Meleah begins to. Nobody doesn't respond, just sits there trembling.

—Nobody, Michael says, his voice loud and stern. I need you to buckle up right now.

She makes a small move in that direction and Meleah reaches over and helps her.

—Stay down, Michael says.

The Brothers are very close now, just a few feet from the tailgate.

—Hold on, Michael says.

He then stomps on the brake pedal and cuts the wheel to the left.

The old Ford screeches to a full stop, laying down a long track of smoke and rubber on the road as it does.

The Brothers come flying past the truck.

As they do, he manages to clip the second bike on the left with the front driver's side quarter panel and edge of the bumper.

The front tire of the motorcycle hits the truck and gets jammed under the bumper, its back end spinning up and slinging the rider off, rider and bike flipping end over end several times.

He's not sure if the crash kills the biker, but he's reasonably sure neither he nor his bike will be able to continue their pursuit.

As the others slow down and start to turn around, he begins moving forward again, rolling down the window and readying the grenade as he does.

The three remaining Brothers and their bikes are now in the center of the highway.

Kicking the stands down and leaning their bikes on them, they climb off and raise their rifles. Assuming a shooter's stance and taking aim, they begin to fire.

Gaining speed.

Heading directly toward them.

Rounds piercing glass and plastic and rusted metal, others ricocheting off the rough surfaces of the old truck.

He has no idea what he's doing.

—Nobody, he says.

She doesn't respond.

—How long after you let go of the lever do these things explode?

—Between two and six Mississippi.

—Err on the short side, Meleah says. What're you gonna do?

—Give it back to the Brothers. Stay down. Hold on. Say a prayer.

—Please be careful.

Keeping his head down as much as possible, Michael risks a glance at the Brothers as rounds fly at him.

Judging they are about fifteen feet away, he lets go of the lever, pauses less than a second, then tosses it out of the window toward the three men.

The shots stop.

He looks up again to see the Brothers scrambling.

But they needn't have bothered.

Not calculating the movement of the truck correctly, Michael has overthrown his target, his heart sinking as he watches the grenade roll right past the Brothers.

—*Fuck!*

—What is it? Meleah asks.

—I threw it too far.

—Fuck, she says.

Figuring it's the only play he has left, Michael floors the gas pedal.

In another couple of seconds, the grenade goes off. It is well beyond the Brothers and has no impact on them or their bikes at all.

They climb to their feet laughing.

Gaining as much speed as possible, Michael drives directly toward the Brothers and their bikes.

The sound of the grenade and the Brothers' preoccupation with it lays cover for the accelerating truck, and so when they are back on their feet again and turning from the grenade back to the truck, he is there.

Still accelerating when he hits them, he manages to reach almost fifty miles per hour.

The front grill and bumper of the truck hits two of the three men directly and clips the other.

The thud and thump of blunt force trauma.

The crack and snap of bones.

The sounds make him sick to his stomach and he swallows hard to keep down the Lefters breakfast he had eaten earlier in the day.

The clang and clatter of guns hitting the asphalt.

Then the metallic scrape and skid and crunch of truck knocking over then running over the motorcycles.

Two of the motorcycles tumble over to the side, but one goes directly beneath the front of the truck, hitting the axle, doing damage to the radiator, scraping along the pavement until it eventually gets wedged and stops the truck.

Throwing the truck into Reverse and punching the gas, he backs up off the bike, cuts his wheels, shoves it back in Drive, and guns the engine again.

Bouncing over bikes and bikers, the truck bucks and sputters but doesn't stop.

—What was that? Meleah asks.

—Best not to know, he says. Y'all stay down just a little longer.

Smoke rising from beneath the hood and out of the air vents makes it difficult to see, and the truck is making a variety of clicks and clunks that lets him know its time rolling down the road is limited.

—Roll down the window, would you? he says.

—Did you get the motherfuckers? Nobody asks as she reaches over and turns the small handle that brings down the glass a little at a time.

A round hits the tailgate.

—Evidently not all of them, he says.

With no mirrors, he has to twist and turn in the seat to see where the shots are coming from.

On the ground, seeming unable to get up, the Brother he had just clipped lies on his side firing at them.

—Stay down, Michael says.

Just a little farther and they'll be out of range. But will the truck make it that far?

Shot to shit. Smoking. Spitting and spurting. The truck is making its protestations both heard and felt, both loud and clear.

He watches in wonderment as the two most important gauges bounce in different directions—the gas gauge toward E, the temperature gauge toward H.

Will it overheat or run out of gas first? Does it matter?

And then the puff of air and rat tat tat of rubber flapping on the road lets him know one of the tires has blown out.

Running on rim.

Not stopping.

—Was that a— Nobody begins.

—Blowout, yeah, he says.

—What're we gonna do? Meleah says.

—I'm gonna ride that rim until it falls off, he says. Or the truck overheats or runs out of gas. We'll get as far away from those fuckers as we can. Then we've got some decisions to make.

2

When he thinks the truck has gone about as far as it's going to go, he turns down a dirt road. Then after unloading everything—including the girls—he drives it into the woods.

If someone is looking for it they'll be able to find it without much effort at all, but they'll have to be looking.

—You think they're still coming after us? Meleah asks.

—I don't think the four bikers are able, but doesn't mean they won't send others once they're able to open the gate. Given the way they were nearly worshipping the Deacon, I'd say they'll want to avenge his death.

—I put you in even more in danger, Nobody says. I didn't even think about that.

—I'm not sure you did, Michael says. Probably would've come after us either way.

—We understand why you did what you did, Meleah says.

Meleah is a counselor specializing in issues relating

to teenage girls. He knows it won't be long before she will be helping Nobody work through her trauma.

—We need to move, Michael says. But we've got to figure out which way and what to do. Let's find a place to hide.

With his backpack and two duffels back in place, he leads them down the dirt road to the highway, then along the fringes of the forest lining 73 until he sees the small wooden house across the street.

—Do you remember this place? he asks Meleah.

She looks at it more closely, then shakes her head.

—One time when we were taking you to see your Grandbob in Atlanta, our car broke down near here. One of the radiator hoses had a hole in it. A very nice elderly Asian couple lived here and helped us repair it.

—I don't remember.

—You were pretty young.

He steps up and knocks on the door.

When he gets no response, he tells the girls to keep an eye on the road while he goes inside.

The door is unlocked. The small, simple house is empty.

He can't imagine the elderly couple had still been alive when the end came, but if they were, he hopes they got out and are somewhere safe.

There is no safe place. They'd be better off below than above ground these days.

—Come on in, he says to the girls. It's empty.

They join him inside the small, musty-smelling structure.

—First, let's check our supplies and see if there's anything useful here. I'm gonna change and go through my bags. Y'all search the kitchen for canned goods, bottled water, anything that's still good. Check the closets for winter gear too. The temperature is dropping fast out there.

Ten minutes later they are sitting around the small, round wooden kitchen table, eating from open cans and packing everything else.

—What decisions do we have to make? Meleah asks.

He's at a loss as to what to do next. He's always been painfully aware that he doesn't know what he's doing, but never as much as at this moment. How can he keep them alive and survive himself while trying to find the others? He's never had a plan beyond finding his family and the friends he can—if they're still around to be found. Now that he's actually found Meleah, what does he do to ensure her safety while searching for the others? What was the use in rescuing her if he can't keep her alive?

—What to do, he says. We've got to figure out the best, safest thing to do with you two.

—What about you? she says. What're you—

—After I get you somewhere safe, I'm going to continue to Wewa to see if anyone else—

—Me too, she says. That's what I want to do. I want to go with you. I want to be with you. And I want to check on everybody too. Taylor. Micah. Mema.

—From all accounts it's only gonna get worse from here. A lot worse. Which is hard to imagine. It's been fairly horrific so far.

—I don't care, Meleah says. I'd rather be in a horrible place with you looking for them than in a safe place—though I'm not sure there is such a thing anymore.

—I'm staying with you too, Nobody says. 'Fraid you're stuck with my crazy ass.

—There's a small community of good people on 73 this side of Marianna, or I could take you to Lynn's, which is probably the best thing to do—except it's pretty bad between here and there. And very dangerous.

—And that would put you even later getting home, Meleah says. You'd be taking unnecessary risks both ways—there and back.

—But—

—It's settled, she says. We're going with you. Unless you think we'll be too big of a burden. Does us being with you mean you won't make it? Will us tagging along make you that much more vulnerable?

Of course it does. It will slow him down, increase his vulnerability, and greatly increase the odds that his mission will fail. But not only can he not tell her that, he really doesn't ever want her out of his sight again. And he certainly can't tell her that.

—Nobody's already proven how valuable she is, he says. And I know how strong and capable you are.

—Can we please call you something besides Nobody? Meleah says.

—I really do prefer it, she says. Much better than my slave name.

—Okay, Michael says, standing. Let's get everything ready and head out. I want each of you to search these drawers for the sharpest knives you can find. Keep one on you at all times. Drink plenty of water. Go to the bathroom. We leave in five.

3

Ragged edge of woods.

Temperature falling fast.

Slow progress.

Tired. Thirsty. Hungry. Cold.

The farther south they go, the colder it gets. It's as if the temperature plummets with every single shivering step they take.

They are bundled up in everything he had and every warm garment they could find at the house, but it's immensely inadequate.

North Florida has seen some cold temperatures over the years, but nothing like this. This is far colder than even the hard freezes that wipe out entire citrus industries.

Michael constantly scans the area around them, turning often to see if they're being followed by any of the Brothers. Or anybody else.

—Be dark soon, he says. Need to find shelter for the night.

—Like what? Meleah asks. Empty house?

—The right one, yeah. But just a structure of some kind. Even the right vehicle. Something to block the wind and keep in some heat.

—Wish we could find another vehicle so we wouldn't have to walk, Nobody says.

—So many places where the road's not passable, he says. Probably wouldn't be able to use it for long anyway.

—Even ten feet is fine with me, she says.

He laughs and starts to say something, when he is struck in the back of the head.

Believing he has been shot, he reaches up to feel for blood as he spins around to see who did it.

—Get down, he yells to the girls as he does.

No one is there. Not visible anyway.

The sniper?

Did he really follow me this far?

He drops down to the ground beside the girls.

How am I still functioning? Was I just grazed?

His hand feels wet, but when he looks at it, no blood is present.

He realizes why when he's struck again. And again. And again.

—It's hail, he says. Thought someone was shooting at us. Come on. Let's find cover.

They scramble to their feet and begin to run.

Out of the woods now. On the road.

Running.

Pellets.

Painful.

Pelting.

The barrage of hail increases until they're in a full-blown bombardment of ice bullets.

Thunder.

Lightning.

A hard, cold rain falling alongside the increasingly large hailstones.

He's only ever seen one other hailstorm. Like this one, it came up fast and pounded everything hard, but that one, which had actually cracked the windshield of his truck, was nothing compared to this one.

It's odd to have hail during cold weather like this, but everything about the weather patterns of the wounded planet are odd right now.

The hard, frozen pellets pounding them now are actually leaving marks on their skin, and in a few cases splitting their flesh open, blood running out from the small cuts.

—Look, Meleah says.

Up ahead on the left side of the road is a tin mechanical-looking building on the edge of a pasture.

He had always found the building odd as he had passed by it over the years. There is nothing else on the property, and though it's located in a pasture, the structure looks like a garage or a small hangar instead of a barn.

—Perfect. Head there.

Picking up their pace, they race toward what looks to be the nearest port in this storm.

When they reach it, they can see that both the large garage door and the standard pedestrian door are bolted and locked.

—Stand back, he says.

Withdrawing the 9mm from his bag, he stands to the side and fires pointblank at the padlock.

The round pierces the lock's casing, but the small hole does nothing toward opening it.

He tries again. Another hole. Same results.

—Hey, Nobody yells.

—Yeah?

—I put the bolt cutters in your bag, remember?

He shakes his head and rolls his eyes at himself.

—Forgot. So stupid. Thanks for reminding me.

He removes the bolt cutters, quickly snaps the lock shackle, twists off and discards the lock, and they're inside.

4

The hiss and crackle of a small fire.

Howling wind outside heard beneath slightly raised garage door.

Rain pinging on a tin roof.

Michael and Meleah warming by the fire. Nobody not far away sleeping in a sleeping bag beneath a pile of clothes and rags.

—I still can't believe you found me, Meleah says.

—It was inevitable. Wouldn't have stopped until I did.

—That's what you're going to do for all the others now?

He nods.

—Got nothing else to do, he says.

The building is mostly empty, and though they are speaking softly and facing the partially open door, their voices still echo around them a bit.

Perhaps part of much bigger plans that never developed, the hangar-like structure seems as though it has never been used for much of anything beyond storage. There are quite a few tools and room for vehicle repair, but it appears as if none have ever been done here. There's some random farm equipment—a few troughs, corral panels, electric fence wire, the mower attachment for a small tractor—and not much else. A few empty storage containers and plastic crates and car parts. The biggest find is in the back corner opposite where they sit now—a Yamaha ATV, a full tank of gas in its belly, key in the ignition. Not that it amounts to much for them. No way it could hold all three of them and their gear.

 —Have you written any since this all began? she asks.

 —Not a single word.

 —Think you will?

 —It's hard to imagine, he says. But harder to imagine I won't.

 —Sorry about your books, she says.

The fire before them consists of pages from a couple of his books and what little dry wood they could find, pallets mostly, inside the mostly empty storage hangar.

 —Brought a couple along for that reason.

 —Let me guess. Nicholas Sparks and—

 —Actually, they're pages from out-of-date computer manuals.

 —Out of date as fuck, she says. Out of time. Out of power. No net. No grid. No nothing.

 —Hard to believe something so ubiquitous and central to nearly everything we did before is as useless as every other random piece of metal and plastic.

 —Crazies always said this day was coming, she says. Remember Y2K?

 —Yeah, but like the Deacon they were wrong. It didn't come for the reasons they said it would, doesn't mean what they say it means.

 —Maybe not.

 —*Maybe?*

She smiles.

Her big brown eyes light up and her sweet, mischievous smile sparkles even in the wavy wan orange glow of the small fire.

—The Deacon was very persuasive.

—Shit. I don't have time to detox you and Nobody too. And I was hoping you'd help with her.

—Already on it, she says.

—I've seen. Thank you.

The garage door is open slightly to let the smoke out, but the draft is poor and much of it stays in. It's cold enough that they don't mind.

—What did happen to the world? she asks. Any ideas?

—A few, but that's all they are, he says.

Nobody stirs, says something unintelligible, and rolls over on her side.

—What are they? Meleah asks, lowering her voice even more.

—I think the bizarre weather is a clue. Something global, something environmental happened. More likely several somethings. Maybe it was all the damage we've done. Chemicals. Pollution. Overpopulation. Pesticides finally poisoned us beyond the point of no return. We finally wiped out too many of the bees. Who knows? Somebody could have finally pushed the wrong button and unleashed chemical, biological, or nuclear weapons. Maybe meteors hit somewhere. Maybe some of all that—and more.

She nods and thinks about it.

—We've had a lot of loaded guns pointed at our heads for a long time now, haven't we? she says.

—The other clue is all the death and infection and mutation accounts for whatever's in the woods, whatever was trying to get Gracie back at Lynn's.

—What was that?

He tells her.

—Climate change can't account for that, she says.

—Don't think it can. So there's something else going on. A contagion. An infectious disease that kills some and changes others, maybe. I don't know. Whatever's going on, we're in the early days of it. Probably know more soon. And then wish we didn't.

She frowns and nods, her eyes wandering away as she contemplates the things as a dad he wishes she didn't have to, that she'd never have to.

—The chaos and collapse has enabled many to give in to their uber-selfish and even sociopathic tendencies that were barely restrained before, he says.

She's a psychologist. She's studied human nature. She's intimately acquainted with the mental illnesses, personality disorders, and capacities for depravity human beings are prone to.

—She mentioned being infected, Meleah says. I just can't bring myself to call her Nobody. Do you think she really is? Is she contagious?

—I have no idea—about anything really—but unless whatever it is has a much longer incubation period in some than others, I don't think she is. She's not showing any signs. We'll watch her closely, take care of her the best we can—psychologically and physically. I could be wrong, of course, and if I am and I'm exposing you . . .

—Even if we are—and it's *we*—I wouldn't change anything. Helping who we can is what we do. It was before the lights went out and it still is now.

He nods, thinking how extraordinary his daughter is and how extraordinarily proud of her he is.

—You're a masterpiece, he says. I'm so glad the world still has you.

She smiles and hugs him.

—Get some sleep, she says. You need some bad. I've been getting plenty for a while now. I'll take the first watch.

—You sure?

—Absolutely. Just give me a gun and I'm good to go.

He gets her set up with the small .38 and begins to make his bed.

—Wake me up if you even think you hear anything or if—

—I will.

—Thank you, he says. I'm so proud of you. I love you so much.

—Love you. Night.

—Night.

—Hey, she says. We gonna use the four wheeler tomorrow?

—Even if I could get it cranked, which is highly doubtful, there's no way it could carry all three of us and our gear.

—Ah, she says. Too bad.

Soon he's out. And out hard. Too hard given the current situation and circumstances.

He doesn't move. Doesn't stir. He doesn't relieve Meleah. Doesn't feed the fire.

When he does finally wake the next morning, he finds the fire out, Meleah asleep, and Nobody long gone, vanished in the night the way the previous world had.

5

—**I**'m so sorry, Meleah says. I can't believe I fell asleep.

—It's my fault, Michael says. I was supposed to relieve you.

—Is she really gone? Whatta you think happened to her?

—Let's look around again to make sure.

They do, searching both inside the structure and the area around it.

—She's not here, Meleah says. I can't believe I let this happen. Do you think she was taken or left on her own?

He thinks about it.

—I knew the fire was a risk, he says. May have led them straight to us, but . . .

—What? she says. What is it?

—If she had been taken—especially by the Brothers—hard to imagine they wouldn't take us too. Or take us out. And I don't think we would've both slept through a struggle.

—So she left on her own. Why? She said you were

stuck with her.

He shrugs.

—I don't know, he says. Maybe she felt like a burden or was scared she was going to infect us. Maybe it's just PTSD. She's been through a lot.

—She could've heard us talking last night, Meleah says. Maybe she wasn't asleep.

—We didn't say anything that would make her leave, did we?

—Talked about her infection. The four wheeler not holding all of us.

—But not in any way that would make her feel like she needed to leave. At least I hope she didn't take anything that way. *Shit.*

—What're we gonna do?

He thinks about it, weighing their options. If someone has her or she really doesn't want to be found, it'll be nearly impossible to find her. They could use all their resources and still never locate her. Searching for her could mean they don't get to the others in time—or at all. What if they get hurt or killed while looking for her?

—We have no way of knowing which way she went, he says. It could be in any direction.

—Can't track her?

He laughs.

—No, he says. I can't track her.

She smiles.

—You've picked up other skills, she says. Thought you may have learned that one too.

—We could waste a ton of time looking for her and never find her, he says. It could not only delay us from getting to Wewa, but we could get hurt or killed while doing it if we run into the wrong people.

She nods, but doesn't say anything.

He thinks about the poor girl who had burst out of the FedEx truck. He had failed to save her, had failed to save or even help so many. Here's an opportunity to not only save a life but a soul. She needs someone to give a damn about her, to come looking for her. The risk is great. But so is the reward. But what if by trying to help her he fails to save Dawn or Micah or Travis? They'd all still say the same thing—you've got to try to find her. You've got to.

     —But, he says, I feel like we've got to try.

     She smiles and nods her agreement.

     —Us arriving a day or so later probably won't change anything for Dawn and Micah and the others.

     —Even if it would, she says, they'd tell us to do it.

     —Exactly what I thought. We could give it a day. If we don't find her, we keep moving.

     —Sounds reasonable. We gonna use the four wheeler?

     —Be fools not to.

6

Betting that Nobody wouldn't continue toward Wewa, Michael and Meleah head back in the direction they had come the day before.

It's still cold. Very cold. But there's no hail. No rain. No storm.

The four wheeler makes the traveling far easier and them a far more easy target.

Luckily it had cranked after just a few tries and the right ratio of choke. Otherwise, they'd be walking.

Michael is driving. Meleah is on the seat behind him. Both have weapons out.

Michael is responsible for scanning the front and the right, Meleah the left and the back, but unable to help himself, he occasionally turns and checks behind them.

—*Da-ad*, Meleah says, frustration in her voice. I'm looking back there. Regularly.

—I know. Sorry. But I'm not looking for her so much as threats.

—That's at least a little better. But I'm looking for those too.

Searching.

Not unlike the fire that kept them marginally warmer last night, the ATV is beneficial but comes with a price. Like a signal fire it draws attention to itself.

Michael tries to keep the vehicle at a steady speed, both for safety and to minimize the noise it makes.

This part of 73 is mostly empty, but when the occasional object appears in the road, the four wheeler can quickly and easily negotiate around it.

Random abandoned vehicles.

An upside-down doghouse.

A dryer on its side.

A Christmas tree lying on its side, lights and garland still wrapping it, busted and broken ornaments on the asphalt around it.

The tree reminds him that though it is February now, it was just before Christmas when all this happened.

7

Even with shades on and a bandana tied around the lower half of his face, the cold wind stings his cheeks and causes his eyes to water, and though he blocks most of the wind off Meleah, he can tell from her arms around him that she is freezing.

Like the land, the road is flat, visibility good.

At the top of the only elevation for miles, he stops, removes the binoculars from his bag, and looks across the prairie-like pine lands in every direction.

He scans for any movement at all—both on the road and along the edge of the woods lining it.

He hid most of his gear in the hangar they'd slept in last night and only has a few items, like the binoculars, in one bag that hangs from the handle bars.

He looks again.

There's no sign of her.

—I think we've already gone farther than she could've walked by now, he says.

—Yeah, Meleah says. Was just thinking the same

thing. So where is she?

—Could've gone in a different direction, he says. Could be avoiding the road, walking the woods the way we did. She may have even hidden when she heard us.

She nods slowly, seeming to think about it, scanning the area around them again.

—If it's none of those, he says, somebody could've taken her.

—How about we go a little farther then turn around and call her as we head back?

He nods.

—Sounds good, he says.

8

Like all the others since the end, the day is gray and hazy, its colorlessness bleaching everything out into a faded monochromatic photograph.

Thick, gray low-hanging clouds make the space above them seem more like a ceiling than a sky, and make him feel claustrophobic.

He drives to the point on the horizon that marks the farthest distance he could see through the binoculars before.

Pulling the binoculars out of the bag, he glasses the area again, carefully looking as far as he can see in every direction—down the road both ways and as far into the forest on each shoulder as the density will allow.

Nothing. No sign of her or anyone else.

—It's like she just vanished, Meleah says.

He nods, continuing to look through the binoculars.

—No way she walked this far, he says.

—Head back yelling for her? Meleah asks.

—Okay, but I really need you to hold on tight. We'll

be calling even more attention to ourselves and I may have to take off fast.

    —Will do.

    He puts the binoculars away.

    —Are we really going to yell Nobody? she says.

    —What choice do we have?

9

They drive along, a little faster, calling for Nobody—Michael to the front and left, Meleah to the back and right.

—NOBODY, Michael yells.

—PLEASE COME OUT, Meleah says. WE NEED TO TALK TO YOU.

They keep this up for a few miles.

When they reach the same slight hill as before, he comes to a stop and pulls out the binoculars again.

Slowly scanning the area around them.

Right side. Nothing.

Left side. Nothing.

Behind them. Nothing.

In front of them. Noth—something.

Movement. Slight. But there.

Some two miles up ahead on the left side of the highway. Old, leaning, unpainted wooden barn. Small, elderly black lady on her hands and knees behind it.

He takes a closer look, lingering on the lady and the area around her.

Wrapped in rags, she appears to be unarmed and harmless.

He can't be sure, but it appears as though she's gardening or perhaps burying something small.

—Look, he says to Meleah, handing her the binoculars.

She squints into the eyecups and adjusts the view.

—What am I lookin'— Oh. What's she doing?

—Not sure.

—Looks harmless. We could go ask her if she's seen Nobody.

—And what the hell she's doing out here by herself.

10

She's among the most emaciated individuals he's yet encountered.

Boney black fingers grip a small garden trowel and spade.

Elongated neck. Razor-sharp jawline. Sunken cheeks. Hollow, hooded eyes. Skin so black it's got a blueish hue.

—Got nothin' worth stealin', she says, stepping back, holding up her small implements.

She hasn't been gardening. She's been working her worm bed.

Small damp pile of dirt. Piece of pressboard propped to one side. Compost scraps—browning banana peel, rotting apple core, wilted lettuce.

—We're not here to steal from you, Michael says.

—We're not here to hurt or harm you in any way, Meleah says.

—What y'alls want then?

—How are you surviving out here? Michael asks. Are you on your own?

—Er'body else done dead and gone. Won't be long 'tils I am too.

—Where do you live? Michael asks. What do you eat?

—Gots a little house on a little lake not far from here, she says. Grub worms to catch fish. Sick of fish, but sho beats eatin' worms.

—Bet it does, Meleah says.

—We're looking for a friend of ours, Michael says.

—Teenage girl, Meleah says. Blond hair. Heart tear tattoos on her face.

—Why y'alls lookin' for her?

—She was traveling with us, Meleah says. She left because she thinks she's a burden, but she's not.

—Have you seen her? Michael asks.

She hesitates.

—We won't force her to go with us, Michael says. We'll just make sure she's okay and make sure she knows we want her to, but she's free to do whatever she wants.

—We's all free, she says. In theory. But I ain't seen much what looks like real freedom in a minute or more.

—Have you seen the girl? Michael asks.

She shakes her head.

But before she has finished, Nobody steps out of the barn.

—You came looking for me? she says. But why?

—Why'd you leave?

—Didn't want to infect you. Didn't want to slow you down or get in your way.

—You're not in the way, Michael says. And I really don't believe you're infected. Why do you think you are?

—The Deacon's doctor said I was.

—He lied, Meleah says. You're not infected.

—I killed him, she says. The Deacon. In cold blood. I'm dangerous and unstable.

—No, you're not, Meleah says. You're a strong young woman who fought back. You're brave and nobody can blame you for what you did.

—You can do whatever you like, but we'd like you to stay with us, Michael says.

She bursts into tears. Big wet drops that moisten and animate her tattoo tears.

—I can't believe you really . . . she says, her sobs cutting off her words. No one's ever . . . I can't believe y'all came back for me.

—Does that mean you'll go with us? Meleah says.

Nobody nods, then steps over and hugs Meleah. Hard. Tight. Long.

—Nancy, she says. My name is Nancy.

Michael looks back over at the old lady.

—We're headed to Wewa to find our family and friends. It's going to be a very rough journey but you're welcome to join us. We'll look out for you the best we can.

She shakes her small head.

—Too old to go gallivanting at this point. I'a be content to live out my remaining days right here.

Michael nods.

—Anything we can do for you or help you with before we go?

She shakes her head.

But then reacts as if something has just occurred to her.

—Think you'll be comin' back this way? she asks.

He nods.

—Think y'alls could look in on me and bury me if I'm gone? I really don't want to be eaten.

11

Frozen wasteland.
     Frost on the gray ground.
     Bleak midwinter blizzard.
     Sheets of sleet. Colorless world.
     Shaking and shivering.
     Foggy breath visible with every icy word.
     Robert Frost's "Fire and Ice" haunts him.
     Some say the world will end in fire,
     Some say in ice.
     From what I've tasted of desire
     I hold with those who favor fire.
     But if it had to perish twice,
     I think I know enough of hate
     To say that for destruction ice
     Is also great
     And would suffice.
     They are making their way south on 73.
     The two girls and most of the gear on the ATV, the

man stumbling along beside them.

—Do you think there's any rhyme or reason for who died and who survived? Nancy asks.

Meleah is driving, her hands wrapped in rags, Nancy holding on to her, huddling into her as much as possible.

—Do you mean in some sort of cosmic sense? Michael asks.

He thinks about humanity's search for meaning, for reasons and causes and purposes, and how often in the absence of finding any, others are fabricated.

We want to matter. We want meaning. We desperately want for there to be order beneath the chaos. And sometimes there actually seems to be.

—Nothing like that. Nothing like the Deacon or any other asshole like him would say. I mean like is it just blind fuckin' luck, right place right time sort of thing, or do those who survived have something—I don't know, a gene or something—that those who died didn't?

—I have no idea, he says. It's a fascinating question. Are we immune in some way or just haven't been exposed yet? Or . . .

—Or what? Nancy asks. What were you going to say?

—I don't know.

—You just don't want to say it in front of us, she says.

—No, I really just forgot what I was going to say. The truth is I just don't know.

—And what about the others? Meleah says. The ones who've been altered, infected—whatever it is? Are we just as susceptible as them, we just haven't come in contact with the contagion yet?

Michael shrugs, which with the way he's shaking and shivering looks more like the gyration of a dance move than a gesture.

—I have no idea. It does seem as though most of the things that appear random at first . . . have some sort of underlying order and pattern waiting to be discovered.

I saw people in Atlanta come into direct contact with the exact same things. Some would live. Some would die. Some would change.

—Into what? Nancy asks. What happens when they . . . transform?

—Not sure exactly. Never been around any of them for long. But I don't think it's just one thing. Agitated. Aggressive. Animalistic. The ones I saw in Atlanta were different from the ones I saw in the woods next to Lynn's.

—I figured they'd get me tonight, she says. Knew I couldn't make it out there on my own. Still can't believe y'all came back for me. I figured you took me with you in the first place so you could fuck me.

—What?

—Originally. I thought you brought me along so you could fuck me or use me as some sort of . . . I don't know . . . decoy or sacrifice or . . . but I see the way you act, the way you treat your daughter, the way you talk about your wife.

Michael shakes his head.

—It was your frame of reference, Meleah says. We understand. But he's not like that. We're not like that.

—Oh, I know now. But . . . the Deacon didn't just start usin' and abusin' me when the end came.

Meleah nodded.

—Most people in the world aren't like that, Michael says.

—Even in this world? Nancy says.

He thinks about it. Fear and chaos and desperation and the uncertainty of survival have brought out the baser instincts and brutality of many who remain. Selfishness and antisocial behavior are rampant. But he still believes there are more decent people than not.

—Even in this one, he says.

—I don't think so, she says. Maybe everybody's not a rapist or a murderer, but . . . they're gonna look out for them and theirs and fuck you and yours. It's why what y'all did is so . . .

—We're not the only ones who would, Meleah says. But you're right, it's probably far fewer than Dad wants to think. Definitely fewer than it should be.

He laughs.

—So I'm the naive one of the group? he says.

—You've always been the glass-half-full guy.

—Guess I have, but . . . Extreme circumstances and situations bring out the extremes in us, sure, but they have to be in us to begin with.

—You were a prison chaplain, she says. You know the extremes that are in us.

—But think about them as a percentage of the population, he says. Was pretty small.

—Yeah, under good circumstances in the richest nation on the planet, not the bleak, brutal world that exists now.

12

Up ahead. Figure standing in the road.

Beyond him, about fifty feet back, a line of vehicles, all headed this way, all fleeing the direction they are traveling in.

Meleah looks over at her dad, tears from the cold trickling down her rash-red cheeks.

He nods and they continue.

As they get closer, he motions for her to slow down a little and let him take the lead.

—Keep an eye out behind us, he tells girls. And beside. Keep checking the woods.

They're both shivering so badly it's difficult to distinguish their nods from their cold-induced movements.

Got to find shelter. Got to get warm.

When he's within thirty feet or so of the man standing in the road, he can see that he's dead.

Frozen in mid-stride.

Early twenties.

Shorts. Flip flops. T-shirt.

Frost covering his clothes and skin. Flakes of ice

clinging to his eyelashes.

How is he still standing?

How is any of this happening?

Good point.

—Is he dead? Nancy asks. Frozen to death?

—He's dead, but he didn't freeze to death. It's cold but not nearly that cold. I think the temperature has nothing to do with what killed him or what's keeping him up. But I really don't know.

—Are you sure he's dead? Meleah says.

—Pretty sure.

She nods and they continue, making a wide berth around the man.

The lane beside the line of cars is mostly empty and they travel down it slowly, eyeing the vehicles as they do.

Cop car. Sideways across the highway. Road block. State trooper leaning in the window of the first car.

Most of the vehicles have drivers and passengers in them. All sitting up, all appearing to be frozen—as if in a three-dimensional photograph. All dead.

Lifeless eyes open.

Expressions eerily animating their lifeless faces.

No blood. No signs of violence.

Bumper to bumper. As if the first car was put in park and held the line as the driver of each car behind died, releasing the brake, causing the vehicle to roll into the one in front of it.

—How is this possible? Meleah asks.

—No idea, Michael says.

—It's one of the most surreal things I've ever seen.

—It's creepy as fuck, Nancy says. I keep expecting them to come to life and jump at us.

13

Trudging on.

Tromping along in the wet coldness, sleet swirling around them, slush on the gray ground.

Pausing at every passing farmhouse. Respite from the damp frigidity, search for essential supplies. Canned food. Bottled water. Warm, dry clothes. Gas for the ATV.

Between stops. Bitter. Bleak. Numbness.

—Can we stop for the night at the next place? Meleah asks. Build a fire. Get dry and warm? Get some sleep?

—Sure, he says. The very next one we come to.

—Can't come soon enough to suit me, Nancy says. I feel like I've got frostbite over my entire body.

More vehicles. These abandoned.

He turns the ignition of each one. Gets nothing but clicks in most cases. Gets nothing in others.

More random objects in the road.

Jukebox. Busted vanity with broken mirror. Metal shelving of a kind not dissimilar to what's in his dad's old hardware store. A Rebel flag raincoat.

—You're not even gonna see if it fits, are you? Meleah says.

He shakes his head.

She smiles.

—Because of what's on it? Nancy asks.

He gives the slightest of nods, not slowing in the least.

In the dreary distance a dingy mailbox at the end of a tree-lined dirt driveway.

Meleah glances over at him and he nods.

Unable to help herself, she speeds up a little, obviously anxious for something resembling dry warmth.

He is able to keep up, but it's an effort.

The dirt drive leading up a quarter mile or more to the property is rock flecked and pocked with icy mud holes.

Tiny white farm house, faded red barn beyond.

Parking the ATV behind the house, they walk back around to the front and enter through the unlocked door.

The pungent odor greeting them isn't death but it's nearly as unpleasant.

The little living room they enter is empty save for a single leather recliner on one wall and an old wooden wardrobe on the other opposite it.

—Wait here and let me take a look around, he says.

9mm drawn, he moves out of the living room and into the kitchen.

Small galley-style kitchen. Empty countertops and sink. Ancient GE appliances he doesn't open.

Short hallway. Tiny bathroom with a claw-foot tub and pedestal sink. Surprisingly big bedroom. King-sized unmade bed. Single nightstand, black Bible, and empty mason jar in the gathered dust atop it. Old house, no closets. Another old wooden wardrobe. And the singular smell of BO.

How long does body odor linger? Maybe it's baked in, as much a part of the place as the clapboards it's constructed with. Or maybe someone is living here and is out foraging or in the barn working.

Not worth the risk. Need to press on.

—I know you don't want to hear this, he yells to the girls, but unfortunately we've got to find another place. Sorry.

A tremor running the length of him leads to a shudder when he gets no response.

Gun not only drawn but cocked and ready, he heads back down the hallway, acutely aware of the creaks in the old boards this time.

Odor stronger now.

Behind him.

Turning . . . too late.

Barrel pressed to the base of his skull.

—What're y'all doin' in my house?

Foul breath even worse than the eye-watering musk and funk of the unbathed body.

—We thought it was empty, Michael says. Abandoned. Didn't realize anyone still lived here. We'll leave right away.

—The hell you will, he says. Not before you pay the piper.

So stupid.

You are. You're too stupid to live.

Why didn't you leave the girls outside? Why didn't you come in alone to check out things first? How could you be so fuckin' careless with Meleah? Why rescue her at all if you were just going to get her hurt or killed in another way?

He starts to say something, but stops to swipe at a bug bite at the back of his neck.

The tips of his fingers graze the syringe, knocking it down to bounce on the hardwood floor.

Strong jolt of something in his veins.

Knees buckling.

Loss of consciousness before he hits the floor.

14

Heavy headed.

Blinking lids. Blurry vision.

When he's finally able to open his eyes, his head is thick, his mouth dry.

Steel workers banging on a ship's keel inside his skull.

Stiff. Sore. Slow.

Unable to move.

Thoughts . . . coming . . . too . . . Brain's not . . . working. Thoughts . . . not . . . coming . . . fast . . . enough.

Blank wall before him.

Flicker of flame. Candlelight providing what little illumination there is.

Hands cuffed behind him.

Standing.

Strapped to . . . something . . . What . . . is it?

He tries to move his eyes around to see what . . .

So sleepy.

Let me just close my eyes for a few more . . .

NO! Wake up. Now. Do you hear me? Wake the fuck up. NOW!

He opens his eyes again. Blinks and licks his lips.

His nose is itching but he is unable to scratch it, and it's bugging the shit out of him.

Focus. Figure out where you are, what's going on.

His cheek hurts like hell. Must have landed on the same spot he'd hit the tree near Lynn's treehouse.

Concentrate.

He's standing on something. A . . . small metal . . . He's strapped to the same thing he's standing on. What is it?

He strains to look.

Where's Meleah? What happened to her and Nancy?

It's a . . . he's standing on and strapped to a . . . large . . . hand truck. Like the ones he used to move refrigerators in his dad's hardware and appliance store growing up.

He's on a hand truck facing the wall. Where?

He tries to . . . It's no good. He can't see around him.

You're naked.

In his slow thick-headedness he hadn't noticed that he doesn't have any clothes on.

I'm naked. Wow. That's not good.

No, it's not. It's also not good it took you so long to realize it.

A door opens behind him.

Someone lumbers into the room.

Based on the smell, it's the same man from before.

—Have a good nap, sweetheart?

Grabbing the hand truck by the handles, the man jerks on it.

Michael feels like he's falling.

Leaned back as if on an incline board, Michael is rolled across the room, through the door, into and down the dark hallway, and back to the living room.

More candles here. Marginally brighter. But everything seen in the flickering gaslight glow of gold and brandy, as if they are trapped inside a giant whiskey bottle.

After the man stands the hand truck beside the recliner, he comes out from behind it to give Michael his first look at him.

He's a big man. But fat too. Massive forearms. Meaty hands. Huge neck and head. Fat face, black rimmed with stubble and grime. Soiled jeans that barely fit and a John Deere T-shirt that leaves the bottom part of his pale, fat, hairy belly showing, his doughy flesh spilling out like a busted can of biscuits.

Across the room the doors of the wardrobe are open. Gutted and retrofitted, the wardrobe is completely empty except for two sets of handcuffs and leg irons mounted to reinforcement boards inside.

Meleah and Nancy, naked and shivering, are imprisoned within the torture closet the wardrobe has become. Tears streak down Meleah's face. Next to her, Nancy's face is a mask of rage.

So pale. So skinny. So exposed. So very naked.

They look so vulnerable, so pathetic and powerless.

He's so overwhelmed he feels the urge to vomit and burst into tears at the same time.

Don't you dare do either, damn you. You did this. *You.* Don't make it worse. Don't you dare.

After making sure both girls are unharmed, he averts his gaze. Not only is it awkward and embarrassing for him to be naked in front of them, and them, him, but he finds it especially painful since from the moment she arrived in the world, Meleah has always been the most modest person he knows.

He tries to say he's sorry, but realizes there's something in his mouth. A gag.

A quick glance over at the girls confirms they're gagged too.

Still believe there are more good people than bad left in the world?

The huge man's labored breathing can be heard coming from the kitchen now. So can his rummaging through the drawers. Both of which halt abruptly.

The enormous man appears in the entranceway of the living room. He is short and squat but has unusually long arms—a feature that adds to the simian quality of his mannerisms and movements. All of which are seen through the shifting flicker of candlelight.

He trundles over to stand in front of the girls.

With his huge, filthy hands he reaches toward them as they begin to squirm and protest, their muffled moans and groans and cries seeming to spur him on.

Michael fights against his restraints and yells into his gag. Neither of which has any effect on the ape-like man.

He paws at them with his big meaty hands, groping, fondling, caressing.

The grunts and groans he makes as he molests the girls are a sick mixture of childlike glee and the sad, sadistic murmurs of an impotent old man.

Michael's stomach lurches and he throws up in his gag and begins to choke.

If the cruel creature hears Michael choking he gives no indication, but he stops when there's a loud knock at the door, hesitating a moment before beginning to lumber over toward it.

—Git your ass in here, you fuckin' faggot, he says as he opens the door. Boy have I got a surprise for you.

He lopes back a little and to the side, and an extremely tall, thin young man enters the room.

At least six-six, he has to duck beneath the door frame.

Long, straight, dirty blond hair. Long, bony fingers. Severe features. Prominent nose. Jutting chin at the end of a razor-sharp jawline.

A wicked delight creeps into his eyes and a lascivious smile wriggles across his lips as he sees Meleah, Nancy, and Michael.

—Candlelight makes it kinda romantic, he says.

Michael has his choking under control, his throat burning from where he swallowed the bile and vomit back down.

—You didn't tell me you got two girls, he says.

—'Cause you got no interest in girls, the ape responds.

—Maybe not to fuck, but to eat. I prefer eating girls. And these look young and tender.

—Well, anyway, the ape man says, they're mine. I'm gonna eat one and keep one to fuck.

Michael's heart drops to pound in his unsettled stomach.

He looks over at Meleah, his helpless, enraged eyes locking onto hers. She looks so scared, so sick and frightened.

Michael quickly changes his expression to one of sympathy and reassurance, though it feels false and futile to do it.

—Which for which? the skinny man asks.

—Really want to keep the brown-haired beauty, but I'm sorta scared to eat the blond bitch. She's kinda skeevy looking, ain't she? Keep her to fuck—I can suit up when I'm havin' my fun with her. Got no rubber to protect my belly if I eat her, though. But it's a shame . . . that brown-eyed bitch is fine as fuck. Look at that son of a bitch, would you? Even a fudge packer like yourself has to see what I mean.

The fat, disgusting baboon is talking about his daughter, the one young woman in all the world who would always be his little girl. Talking about all of them in ways no human beings should ever talk or be talked about.

—How the hell'd you get all three of them off the road and up here?

—Came up here of their own accord, he says. Didn't have to do a damn . . .

Seeming to lose interest with the fat man's prattle, the tall man walks over to examine Michael more closely.

Pulling out a penlight, he inspects every inch of the man's nude body.

—Smells like puke, he says.

Michael has never been naked in front of another

man before, and to have them not only looking at but inspecting him makes him feel more exposed, more vulnerable, more truly nude than at any other time in his entire life.

—Do we got a deal? the squat man asks, coming up behind him.

—How much for the man and one of the girls?

—Throw in the generator and you can have half a girl.

They're talking about rape and murder and cannibalism in such a casual, matter-of-fact way, it's the most surreal conversation he's ever heard.

How else would people like them talk about it?

Is this really happening?

Yes it is, and for you and your daughter and that poor child you thought you saved, this is the way the world ends.

He can see no way out of this. No help. No hope.

Meleah would've been better off with the Deacon. Nancy was doing better where she was. All you've done is deliver them into torture and an unimaginably horrific short life before certain death.

I can't have. This can't be happening. Wake up. Wake the fuck up.

You're awake. This is your reality now—and the reality of your daughter and the damaged girl you got to help you.

—Tol' you, the generator's not an option, the tall skinny man says.

—Okay then. No deal. Second thought, think I'll just keep the man too. Wait 'til I can get a better deal or just eat him too.

—Wait a minute now . . . Don't be like that. We always deal. Remember that plump brown thing I found you a few weeks back.

—I paid you plenty for that and it wasn't right no way. Felt funny when I fucked her and tasted funny when I ate her.

—I had no way of knowing that. It was a good faith

deal. Tell you what . . . I'll refund you for the plumper and pay what you want for the man and I'll forget all about the girls. Deal?

  —I don't know.

  —Come on man.

  —Got my heart set on that generator now.

  —Fuck man. Okay. The generator for the man and half a girl.

  —No. The price we agreed on *plus* the generator.

  —Shit. Okay. Wait 'til I have something you really want.

  The fat man spits on his huge hand and extends it. The skinny man repeats the same action and they shake.

  The tall, thin man wastes no time taking possession of his new purchase, and within minutes he is wheeling Michael out on the hand truck. Michael's too thin, too pale naked body lying at an incline, being snatched and jerked as it moves across the room.

  Nancy is jerking against her chains, yelling at the men.

  Meleah is crying, her big brown eyes the most sad and frightened he's ever seen them.

  He can't even think about the horrific fate awaiting him for worrying about what his little girl is about to go through. What his actions have brought down on her.

  As he's pulled through the door, she's crying harder now and yelling and screaming through her gag.

  —I love you so much, he tries to say. I'm so sorry. I'm so, so sorry. Please forgive me.

  His gag prevents her from hearing his words.

  But her gag doesn't prevent him from hearing her muffled screams even after the door is closed and he's being rolled naked through the icy darkness, the final image of his good, kind daughter, tearful and terrified, helpless and exposed, begging and pleading for his help, the nasty simian creature sidling up to her forever seared in his memory.

Part 5
The Long Dark Night

1

Meleah has exhausted herself trying to come up with something to do, some way to save them.

There is nothing. Or if there is, she can't come up with it.

Beside her, Nancy struggles against her restraints. She had done the same for a while—until she figured out how futile it was.

The world ends every day. For somebody. This is how it ends for her and her dad and the poor creature who had helped her escape the Deacon.

She can think of better ways to die, but in the end death is death.

After you're gone, does any of it matter anyway?

But what about before then? What about the things these sociopaths plan to do with them before they kill them?

Degradation. Violation. Humiliation. And pain. Lots of pain.

Of course, the real terror is in what they'll do to her dad. That and waiting for all of it.

It's a grace that they've separated us. He doesn't have to witness what they're going to do to me and I don't have to witness what they're going to do to him. The imagining is bad enough.

Think of something else.

Breathe.

Get control of your mind. You can do it.

Accept what is. Breathe in peace. Let go of what you can't control. Gently control what you can—your mind.

She gives thanks for her life. For her family. For Dad, Mom, Micah, Travis. Taylor. Mema. Papa.

We had such a great life. So very much to be grateful for.

Did any of them survive? Are they still alive? Are they somewhere safe? God, she wishes they could all be. Together. Safe. Healthy. Hell, she'd settle for just all being together again.

Thinking of her family fills her with a peace and warmth that seems impossible given her predicament, but there it is.

Everything is fleeting. Everything is temporary. Whatever pain there is, whatever suffering there will be, won't last—not forever.

2

Blind rage.

Nancy has experienced extreme anger before—many times—but this . . . this is something different. Something new.

She literally can't see.

She can't really think straight either.

But boy can she feel. She can feel like a motherfucker. And what she feels—*all* she feels right now—is bright, blinding fuckin' fury.

Not only is the feeling overwhelming everything else, it's actually overtaking her. She's coming undone as she becomes pure rage.

Bits of her psyche are breaking off.

Her humanity is disintegrating. The beast beneath unleashed.

Nancy is no longer Nancy. She's Nobody again.

But no matter who she is or is not, she is not going to be touched by another sick fuckin' prick as along as she lives—neither as fuck hole nor food.

She pulls against her restraints.

Hard.

It helps that they are on a chain bolted to boards in the wardrobe. Gives her leverage. Something to pull against. Helps make what she's about to do possible.

She has very, very small hands. It may take dislocating her thumb or worse, but her hands are coming through the cuffs. She'll break bones and scrape her skin off if she has to, but her goddamn hands are coming through these goddamn cuffs.

Beside her Meleah is crying, a certain hopeless dread in her frightened eyes, her entire face a mask of fear.

Michael has just been rolled out, the door closed behind him, and the fat disgusting fuck is waddling their way—something she knows because she can smell him.

Pull!

She pulls even more feverishly, folding her tiny hand even more, its shape contorting to the point of deformity.

As the ape nears her, he slowly fades into focus as her vision begins to return.

In the flicker of the candlelight, his movements look like those of the old black-and-white movie monsters her mother used to watch late at night.

God, she misses her mommy.

Pretend like he has your mommy and you have to kill him to get her back.

His thick, pink tongue is protruding from his crusty mouth.

Motherfucker is literally licking his lips.

She yells and screams in her gag and pulls even more frantically on her restraints.

—You're makin' me so fuckin' hard, he says between nasally labored breaths. Can't wait to take that shit out of your mouth and really hear you.

He leans his huge repellent head into her and begins to sniff and lick her body. Her neck. Her nipples.

Meleah, who is no longer crying, begins to fight against her restraints too.

—Struggle all you want, he says, his putrid breath hurting Nancy's nose. Won't do y'all any good, but sure as hell gets me goin'.

They continue railing against their restraints.

—Bigger, stronger bitches than y'all haven't been able to break out.

His flabby, odious tongue trails across her cheek and into her ear, then back over her face and into her nostrils.

Grabbing her the bottom of her left arm, he lifts it and begins to lick beneath it, smelling and lapping her armpit like a rare delicacy.

If all of this weren't enough, he begins to move his other hand over her body, roughly grabbing each breast, pinching each nipple between dirty, callused fingers, until to her horror, he slides it down her tummy and between her legs.

When his stubby, fat finger enters her, she goes blind with rage again.

3

Nocturnal noises.

Shrill. Inhuman. Shrieks.

Out of the cold darkness, from the woods surrounding the small house of horrors and the barn behind it, he hears a more intense iteration of the terrifying sounds he's heard in all the woods along his way.

—Sound closer tonight, the tall man pulling him along in the hand truck says. Or at least louder.

The dolly bounces across the cold, hard, damp yard, jarring Michael's naked body strapped to it as it does.

Think!

He's always valued his mind. Used it to create and figure and deduce. Before this moment he thought it was his strength—his ability to problem solve and suss out solutions—but right now he can't come up with anything. Not anything at all.

Your daughter is back in the house with that vile baboon and you can't come up with a way to save her. Nothing? No ideas at all?

He's never felt as useless, as weak and powerless, in his entire life.

Maybe you can't come up with a way out of this because there is no way out.

It can't be. There's got to be something. Some way to . . .

I'm afraid this scene has already been scripted, partner. Nothing to do but play your part. Every conflict has casualties. Nobody ever wants to be one, but somebody's got to.

—Fat fuck really thinks he's gonna get my generator, the tall man is saying. Fuck that. Fuck him. Put his fat ass down. Keep my generator and take his shit too. That's the new deal, bitch. Spit in your fat, stubby-fingered hand and shake on that. What? Oh, you can't cause you're dead. Oh.

Reaching the truck, the man stands Michael up, steps around, and opens the tailgate, letting it drop loudly.

He then turns to look at his prisoner.

—Cold as shit, ain't it. I'll warm you up. Just let me finish a little business first and I'll get you good and hot. Make that ass burn like it's on fire.

Reaching up with the cold, bony fingers of his long, skinny hand, he holds Michael's cheek the way a lover would.

—We're gonna have some fun, he says. Well, one of us is. Guess which one. You get two guesses and the first one don't count.

Dropping his hand, he moves around to the back of the hand truck again, rubbing Michael's thigh with his fingertips as he does.

—Let's get you loaded, finish up, and get the fuck out of here. Ready to be back at my place with you.

He leans Michael down again, spins the dolly around, then props it across the tailgate.

Climbing up into the truck he pulls the dolly in.

Lowering the cart onto the bed of the truck, he climbs back down and closes the tailgate.

Lying flat on the dolly inside the bed of the truck,

Michael can see nothing. But he can hear plenty.

He hears the piercing shrieks of the inhuman. Hears the tall man walk around to the front of the truck and open the door.

Both the dome and cargo lights come on, providing a momentary respite from the relentless dark.

Though weak and dim, the small lights blind him at first, but as his eyes adjust he can see that the tall man is removing a rifle from the gun rack across the back window.

Then the door closes.

Dark again.

No sight, only sound.

The tall man making his way back toward the house.

Do something.

He pulls against his restraints, tugging at them with all his remaining might.

Like what?

Whatever you have to.

He tries forcing his hand through the cuff. It won't give.

It occurs to him that if he dislocates his thumb he might be able to break enough bones to get his hand through the cuff.

Then what? What're you gonna do with one free broken hand?

Figure that out when I get to it.

You're being foolish as fuck.

Gotta do something.

Sure. So why not futilely break your hand, right?

4

Rage.

Brilliant. Blinding. Red. Rage.

She actually sees the color red.

Suddenly the fat fuck before her becomes the Deacon and every other man and boy who has ever forced himself on her, who has ever felt her up, groped her, fingered her, molested her, raped her, or in any way used her for their selfish fuckin' pleasure.

She pulls so hard on the cuff that, though her hand doesn't slip through it, the eyebolt splinters the wood and breaks free from the board, slinging out and hitting her in the back.

Her hands are still cuffed together but are free from the back wall of the wardrobe.

The ape is so lost in his violation and molestation of her, he doesn't realize what is going on.

Bringing her hands up her sides and over her head, she wraps the chain around the fat disgusting fuck's neck and begins to pull in opposite directions as hard as she possibly can.

Inhumanly hard.

Snatching his short, fat finger out of her, he brings his hands up to grab at the chain choking him, but can't get his stubby sausages under it.

The flesh of his fat neck bulges out over both sides of the chain and in-between the circle of each link.

She pulls even harder, the force she's using that of several men bigger and stronger than her.

The ape coughs and chokes and gasps for air he can't get.

Realizing the pointlessness of trying for the chain, the fat fuck begins to twist and jerk, attempting to wriggle out, but this too is utterly ineffective.

He then begins to hit her.

Flinging his fat arms and big fists back at her.

Hard, heavy blows.

He lands shots on her shoulders, chest, jaw, forehead.

Each hit hurts like hell, but she doesn't let go, doesn't let up, doesn't stop choking the life out of this rabid animal that should've been put down years ago, should've been aborted by his wretched mother or an intelligent universe but was not. She's having to do what they could not or did not. But how much damage has he done between then and now?

He tries to speak but only gurgling sounds escape his repulsive mouth.

As he weakens, his punches become more looping and less effective, fewer of them landing.

This might just work. We may just survive this yet.

She's actually feeling somewhat hopeful.

Until the door bursts open.

5

Futility.

The cuffs are so tight, his hands so much bigger and wider than his wrists, he can't possibly pull free—no matter how many bones he's willing to break.

Helpless.

There's nothing he can do but lie here in the dark. Cold. Naked. Afraid.

Two dangerous and deranged men with demented appetites have his daughter and all he can do is shiver in the dark as he strains to hear what's happening.

And he can't even really do that.

No matter how much he tries to hear what's happening in the house, all he can hear are the cries and screams, shrieks and screeches coming from the forest.

Or are they?

They sound closer than that.

A lot closer.

Screeches. Squeals. Squawks. All swirl around him in the absolute black that is the sightless night.

Beyond night blind.

Darker than dark. Blacker than black.

Memory from childhood. Touring the Florida Caverns. Underground limestone caves near Marianna. Deep beneath the huge rock formations. No natural light. No lost light. Tour guide turns off the lights. Nothing but blackness. The darkest dark he's ever seen before the end, before the way the world is now. Now it's darker somehow.

It's so dark, so completely devoid of visibility, he begins to see things.

The terrifying sounds in his ears cause him to see creatures that aren't there, that only exist within his noise-inspired imagination.

Whatever's out there is human. Altered. Changed. Transformed. But human. Not creature. Not monster. Not anything like the imaginings of books and movies before the end began.

And then *WHAM!*

Something strikes the side of the truck.

Hard blow. Rocking the truck on its springs.

And then an inhuman sound somewhere between a shrill caw and a shrieking roar.

What the hell was that?

One of the inhumans? Are these different than the others he's encountered? Altered by the events at the end in ways the others weren't? Maybe the closer you get to the Gulf, the more fully transformation has occurred.

If that's what it is . . . Are they really that close? What else can it be?

He's never heard anything like it before. Anywhere. Ever.

Have they really come out of the woods?

It's not that far out.

No, but farther out than he's ever seen or even heard of.

He remains perfectly still.

Still no shot.

Surely the tall man is in the house by now, but he

had expected to hear a shot and hasn't.

What's he waiting on? Did he make a different deal with the ape man? Or did he just not hear the shot for all the noise out here?

Is he just going to kill the fat man, or the girls too?

He pictures the tall man dropping the lifeless bodies of Meleah and Nancy in the back with him, him having to ride to the tall man's place with his dead daughter next to him.

Suddenly he can't breathe. He can't move.

Frozen in the fear that horrific thought produces, he's unable to function.

His chest and arms ache like he's having a heart attack.

Am I dying?

Maybe it's best if you all do. Now instead of later. Not have to endure any of the unimaginable horror awaiting each of you.

Maybe it is.

6

The fat man is almost unconscious when the door slings open and the tall man is standing there, his rifle pointed at them.

With his last gasp of breath and his last bit of strength, the ape-like creature reaches out for the tall man pointing the gun in his direction.

His dirty, swollen, hairy forearm is right there in front of Meleah's face. She'd bite it if she wasn't gagged. She strains to spit the gag out of her mouth, working her tongue hard against the filthy rag.

—He-el-p me, he manages to get out in a breathy, barely audible plea.

—How the hell'd you let that little pixie runt get the jump on you?

The tall man sounds more amused than anything else, and makes no move to help the dying ape.

—You're about a worthless fat sack of shit, ain't ya? A little girl like that takin' you out—and her anorexic ass still chained up. Goddamn but this is the most entertaining thing I've seen in a by god while. Promise you that.

He starts to step into the room for a better view—but a noise in the yard causes him to jerk his head around and aim his rifle out into the darkness.

—The fuck?

He strains to see out into the black.

—No way you got free of those—

Something from the dark grabs the barrel of the rifle and snatches him out into the darkness.

The tall man screams. Fires a round. Then screams some more.

The shrieks and shrills and screeches grow louder, reaching a fevered pitch in what sounds like a feeding frenzy.

Teeth tearing flesh. Bones cracking and snapping and popping. Wet thumps and slurps and chews.

Back inside, the fat fuck goes limp, the weight of him pulling Nancy forward. She starts to unwrap the chain from around his neck.

Meleah finally manages to get part of the gag out of her mouth—enough to utter muffled words.

—Wait, she says, realizing he might not be dead yet.

—What?

—Don't let go of him yet. And look in his pockets for a key.

With what appears to be all her might, she pulls up on the cuffs, attempting to draw the man and his pockets closer, but it's no use. His dead weight doesn't budge.

—Hurry, Meleah says. We've got to get Dad before those things do.

—We can't go out there, Nancy says.

The hell we can't.

With the chain still around the fat man's fat neck, she searches the pockets she can reach, her small, swollen hands in obvious pain as she does.

—They're not here.

—Can you reach the other side? Meleah asks.

So far she has only reached inside the front pocket

closest to her.

—I don't think I can, but there's a pocket knife in this one. Maybe we can . . .

—Hold on to the knife, but try the other pockets. Hurry.

The horrific noises from the dark yard persist.

Will they come in here? Do they already have Dad? Are they really eating the tall man? Is that really what we're hearing?

—No key, Nancy says. I've gone through all the pockets but one. It's in the back and I've never known anyone to keep keys in their back pocket.

—Are you okay? Meleah asks.

—Whatta you—

Before she can finish, the large man's arms shoot up and grab her by the neck.

Meleah jumps.

Nancy tries to pull on the chain looped around the Neanderthal's neck, but it's no good. He has her now. His grip is stronger and he's not letting go.

Even in his weakened state, his huge hands are easily collapsing her neck, crushing her windpipe.

She looks as though she's about to pass out.

They were so close to being free of the two reptilian men, and then this.

It's mere moments before he kills her and then he'll be on to me.

But then something else happens.

Nancy lets go of the chain, releasing her only leverage on the fat man, as if she's giving in completely, surrendering to the inevitability of her demise.

Then just as suddenly as the man had grabbed her, Nancy is stabbing him with his own knife. Stabbing and hacking and slicing and cutting.

In a few big heartbeats blood is spurting out of large, open wounds, seeping out of smaller ones.

Yellow fat and blood and water gushes out of a long incision in his side.

Releasing his grip on her throat, he reaches to hold his cuts and try to push back in what is coming out of him as he rolls, attempting to get away from her.

He's nearly clear of her, but just before he makes it beyond her reach, she jabs the blade into the side of his neck. Once. Twice. Three quick stabs.

Arterial spray goes everywhere, splattering the floor and ceiling and everything in between that comes in direct line with the wound.

He reaches for it and crawls a few feet away before collapsing to the floor.

He never utters another word. Just rolls around a bit then bleeds out.

—Hey, Meleah says. Look at me. Nancy?

She's obviously in shock or in some sort of dissociative state.

—Hey. Are you okay? Nancy. Look at me.

She finally looks in Meleah's direction, her distant eyes unfocused and glazed over.

—He deserves far worse, she says finally.

Meleah nods.

—Can you use the knife to unbolt your leg irons?

7

A shot.

Screams.

Then . . . what?

He hears what sounds like a man being torn apart. Literally.

Am I next?

What's happening? Are the girls okay?

Was it the fat or tall man? The fact that a shot was fired makes him think it was the tall, man, but it's very likely the fat man has a gun too.

Why are the things out of the woods?

Are they? Think about it. This place is pretty far back from the road. There are woods all around and it's dark as fuck.

Do they know I'm in here? Just keep still. Don't move. Don't breathe.

That would sort of defeat the purpose, now wouldn't it?

You know what I mean. Stay calm and keep quiet.

He feels anything but calm, but he's not moving or making a sound.

Short, shallow breaths. No problem. But his heart is pounding so hard it's making noise and moving his chest.

Calm down. Distract yourself.

If they know he's here and he's about to be attacked and eaten, it'll be over soon, but if they don't and something has happened to one or both of the men, it's going to be a very long, cold night.

Already is.

He's freezing.

He thinks about the long nights in his life.

The recent long nights with his wife. He's had many ecstatic and excruciating nights with Dawn.

Most nights they stay up late together and many nights they've stayed up and or out most of the night.

The Rumi line comes to mind again.

When I am with you, we stay up all night.
When you're not here, I can't go to sleep.
Praise God for those two insomnias!
And the difference between them.

When they first started seeing each other, she lived in a rented trailer on the river. Often, after her fifteen-year-old son went to bed, he'd slip in through the back door that led into her room. They'd make love and then stay entangled as they whispered to each other through most of the night.

After they were married and with each other all night every night, they'd often talk into the early hours, their mouths growing dry, their eyes drowsy as the first light broke above the North Florida slash pines along the eastern horizon.

He thinks about how often they've stayed out late at their bar—Tuck's—or out with friends in Panama City into the wee hours.

How many times have they raided the kitchen in the middle of the night for snacks or to cook something together, or jumped in the car and driven to Waffle House for country ham and hash browns?

There are no Waffle Houses anymore. Not much food. And none to cook. There may not even be a Dawn anymore—or a Michael any moment now.

Though the vast majority of their nights together have been ecstatic, there have been a few that were nothing less than excruciating.

Nights in the hospital—before and after Dawn's back surgeries. Nights at home and in the hospital, him caring for her, her fighting infection so severe her doctor hung the lab report of it on his office wall.

Sleepless nights when she was in too much pain to sleep, when he was exhausted and frayed, but had to do for her everything she couldn't do for herself—which at the time was everything.

Then there were the fight nights. Nights when sleep was sacrificed on the altar of arguments, misunderstandings, hurt, and anger. They were a small fraction of their sleeplessnesses, but they were difficult and painful—and he'd give anything to be back in the middle of one right now.

As this night drags on, he thinks of the many lonely nights before Dawn—those spent in loss and longing.

He had always been a nocturnal creature, had spent the vast majority of his late nights alone, his kids asleep down the hall, most of the rest of the world gone to the underworld of dreams and nightmares.

How many books had he read through those nights? How many movies had he watched? How many prayers had he said? How many books had he written?

He thinks of the times when inspiration kept him up, kept him chasing down the story, his fingers dancing across the keys of the many keyboards he'd worn out over the years.

How many words had he written before the end? Two million? Three? More?

He's had some long nights in his life—both before and since the end—but this one is shaping up to be the longest of them all.

He's never spent a night like this, never been as completely night blind before, never been this close to Meleah without being able to check on her.

In the absolute black of the moonless, starless, lightless night, his eyes are unable to adjust—there is nothing for them to adjust to—and the darkness is as disorienting as anything he's ever experienced.

Plane crashes over the ocean.

He feels like a night pilot over a black sea when the darkness of sky above and sea below become one to the point that the horizon vanishes, and like outer space there is no up or down, no way to navigate, no way to know that you're flying your plane into the wrong bit of blackness, the one that rips your aircraft apart and makes your grave a watery one.

He thinks of other long nights—like the ones of his novels.

Double Exposure and *Blood Moon*.

Two of his novels largely take place over the course of a single night. A long night. The longest of nights—not unlike the one he's experiencing at this moment.

Blood Moon, in his John Jordan series, is the most recent. The love of John's life, Anna, has been kidnapped. He tries to recall how it begins.

> *Waiting.*
> *Alone in the dark.*
> *Thinking.*
> *Praying.*
> *Preparing.*
> *Waiting.*
> *I was waiting for a call—the single most important phone call of my life.*
> *Earlier in the night I had arrived home to find Anna gone.*
> *Not just gone. Taken.*

Would he write again? Would there ever again be a

world in which novels had a place?

He misses writing the way he would if his hand had been chopped off. It was such an essential, core, vital part of him for so long, he feels less himself without the practice of it.

Though *Double Exposure* had been written long before *Blood Moon*, and long, long before all this began, he still remembers much of it. It had been a singular book among the many he had written, the one that had changed so very many things for him, its opening lines the ones he'd read more than any other in his life.

Evening.

Fall. North Florida.

Bruised sky above rusted rim of earth.

Black forest backlit by plum-colored clouds. Receding glow. Expanding dark.

Deep in the cold woods of the Apalachicola River Basin, Remington James slowly makes his way beneath a canopy of pine and oak and cypress trees along a forest floor of fallen pine straw, wishing he'd worn a better jacket, his Chippewa snake boots slipping occasionally, unable to find footing on the slick surface.

Above him, a brisk breeze whistles through the branches, swaying the treetops in an ancient dance, raining down dead leaves and pine needles.

Screams.

He hears what sounds like human screams from a great distance away . . .

He can't help but contrast the long night in *Double Exposure* with this one. Over the course of a single, long night, Remington James is constantly moving, scrambling through the North Florida forest trying to stay alive, whereas he is strapped to a hand truck in the back of a pickup, unable to move, unable to do anything but use his mind in an attempt to quiet and calm his mind.

Remington thought *that* was a long night. Try one like this and get back to me.

Suddenly he's back in the hospital for the birth of his two children. Neither child, Micah nor Meleah, came easily, and both were very long nights, but unlike this one, long nights with activity—Lamaze, walking the maternity wing to try to induce, Pitocin drip, pain, agony, middle of the night decision followed by an epidural. And eventually, sometime later the next day, the arrivals.

Action. Activity.

All the thoughts and memories he's having about previous longest nights ever, both fictional and not, involved him and his characters actually doing something, being able to take action.

Is this what a quadriplegic feels like?

Coming out of his thoughts, returning his attention to the present, he realizes that the shrieks and squeals and screams have receded a bit.

As if by a fader on a soundboard, the overall volume is lower. Their proximity seems farther way too.

Are they leaving? Returning to the woods? Why? Daylight soon or did they destroy everyone?

8

Blinking.

His eyes open. Slowly. Then close against the faint light.

Morning.

Still here. Still naked. Still strapped to a hand truck in the back of a pickup. But still here.

No noises. At least none of the nightmarish nocturnal ones.

A little wind whistles through the pines.

Birdsong.

A solitary bird greets the cold, gray day.

Evidently there are a few animals left. Very few, but some. Augustus's dog Jackson, this bird, the livestock the Lefters had. What else?

Footsteps.

Running.

Bump.

Something gently banging into the side of the truck.

Meleah looking over, smiling down at him.

Then Nancy beside her.

Both their faces blood-speckled and pale, their eyes red-rimmed, worn, weary.

Meleah throws a jacket over him as Nancy climbs in the truck bed with him and begins to unlock his restraints.

—I'm so glad y'all are alive, he says. I had no way of . . . All I could do was listen, but I couldn't hear much of anything over the noise out here. What happened?

Meleah tells him.

He looks at Nancy.

—You're amazing, he says.

She doesn't respond.

—So strong, so incredibly brave. Once again we owe our lives to you.

She still doesn't say anything.

Michael looks back at Meleah.

—It's taken a toll, she says.

He nods.

—Everything has, Meleah says. On us all. But she's been through so much.

Nancy still doesn't say anything.

—I'm so sorry I couldn't protect you, Michael says. That I didn't prevent that from happening or stop it once it did. I feel like I've let y'all down more than anyone ever.

Meleah shakes her head.

—You let me down far more when you divorced Mom, she says.

It's a family joke. He had worked so hard their entire lives to protect them and keep them from all forms of harm and had succeeded—until when they were grown and nearly grown, he had divorced their mom. Far and away the most difficult and challenging event they had experienced. Which as difficult and challenging events go wasn't that horrendous—especially considering the careful, amicable way it unfolded.

She begins to laugh. And he joins her, grateful for the moment of levity.

—Sorry about that too, he says for the thousandth time.

—God, I wish my mom would have divorced my dad and then the damn Deacon, Nancy says.

When he is unstrapped, he sits up and gets dizzy. Using the jacket for cover, he climbs to his feet, various parts of his extremities tingling as they try to wake up.

He extends his hand to help Nancy out of the truck, but she doesn't take it. Instead she pretends she doesn't see it.

Once he's down from the truck, he looks around.

Except for what's left of the tall man, the yard is as empty as it was the day before when they first came upon it.

The body of the tall man is pale and stiff, much of his midsection missing, blood and bile and viscera spilling out of the open cavity and onto the frozen ground around him.

—The fat man still inside? he asks.

—His body, Meleah says.

—We don't have the time or energy to bury them, he says, but we can—

—We're going to burn them, Nancy says. We're gonna burn their goddamn house down around them.

To do so will not only require much needed supplies—particularly gas—and will draw attention they don't need. But obviously she needs to do it, and how can he refuse her this when she's been through so much?

—Okay, he says. Are my bags and the ATV still in the back?

They both nod.

—Let me get dressed and get everything ready so we can get out of here once the deed is done. I'll syphon gas out of the truck and check the barn. There's a pitcher pump in the back. Why don't y'all see if it works and get cleaned up?

—Not quite ready to wash the motherfucker's blood off me just yet, Nancy says.

He nods.

—Would you check the kitchen then? he says. See if there are any canned goods or water?

Without saying anything, she heads in that direction.

—Are you okay? he asks Meleah.

She nods.

—Relatively, she says. Honestly can't believe we're still alive. Thought for sure we were . . .

—Yeah, me too. I love you so much. So glad you're still in the world—even this one. Let's get out of here as fast as we can. And we've got to keep an eye on her. She's in a very bad place.

—If you could've seen what she did . . . There are a lot of things worse than dying—and she's been through most of them.

They walk around to the back of the house. Meleah washes in the water from the pitcher pump as he gets dressed.

In the barn, he finds several cans of gas and ramps he uses to load the ATV into the back of the truck.

He then gathers all the weapons he can find—including the rifle still lying near the remains of the tall man.

Using the dolly he had spent the night strapped to, he hauls what's left of the tall man's body into the house, then he and Nancy spread gas from two of the cans around the rooms and on the bodies.

From the doorway, they take a last look inside.

—Some real bad shit happened, she says. But it coulda been a lot worse.

He nods, then hands her the box of matches and steps back.

She strikes one and tosses it on the fat man first.

Flame. Accelerant. *Poof.* Fire.

She then does the same to what's left of the tall man with similar results.

Next she tosses a few into other parts of the room and through the windows they had opened in other parts of the house.

When she's done, she stumbles over to the pitcher pump and washes the gas and soot and blood off, and joins Michael and Meleah in the truck.

As the three of them ease down the driveway in the cab of the old truck, gas and gear and the ATV in the bed behind them, the house has a good burn going, smoke billowing and flames leaping out of the open doors and windows.

—I don't know what the fuck that is in the woods, Nancy says. Don't know what the fuck is wrong with them, but whatever it is, it's nothing compared to those two sick pricks being roasted in that house back there.

9

They ride in silence.

The old truck easing down the highway.

Their breathing, the close proximity of their bodies in the small cab, and the pickup's heater combine to create a good deal of heat, and they're the warmest they've been since leaving the Lefters.

The wordlessness isn't awkward exactly, but it is rich and resonant, not without something palpable in it.

They are beyond exhausted. Beyond spent. Beyond everything.

Shells of themselves in shock, there's a certain distance and disassociation within their psyches, a defensiveness and coping mechanism, as automatic as oxygen-rich red blood cells rushing to an open wound.

Nancy, still holding the fat man's pocket knife with the blade out, lets out a harsh, humorless laugh.

—Still think there are more good people than bad in this world? she says.

It takes him a while to respond.

—I do, actually. It's anecdotal I know, but I've encountered more decent than destructive people in my travels so far.

She shakes her head.

Meleah smiles.

—He's not as naive as he sounds. And he's probably right, but right now . . . sure doesn't seem like it.

—No it doesn't, he says. It certainly doesn't.

They fall back into silence and stay there.

Eventually, Meleah begins to look around the tall man's truck, beneath and behind the bench seat and in the glovebox.

The search yields very little—some trash, old registration and insurance cards, a can of Vienna sausages, and some ammunition.

She manages a smile when she sees that there's a cassette tape in the player in the dashboard in front of her.

—Wanna guess at the musical tastes of that skinny sick prick? she says.

Nancy doesn't respond.

Michael smiles a little.

—Couldn't begin to imagine, he says.

—Oh, come on. Let's at least give it a try. I say it's Country—something classic like Johnny Cash. How about it?

He tries to decide between metal and religious.

—I'm gonna go with Gospel, he says. Some Southern Gospel family. The Happy Rectums.

—The what?

—You heard me.

Meleah turns to Nancy.

—Not gonna turn it on until you give me a guess, she says.

Nancy sighs but a slight smile trembles her lips.

—It's either gonna be KISS or Lynyrd Skynyrd.

—Ooh, good guess, Meleah says. Okay, whoever gets it or is closest to it . . . gets an extra serving of whatever delicious meal we have tonight.

She then reaches up slowly, her trembling extended finger betraying her attempt at lightening the mood.

When she presses the button and the sound system comes to life, Air Supply's "All Out of Love" in midsong bursts forth to fill the truck.

—Make it stop, Michael says. Make it stop.

She does.

—That's by far the worst thing I've encountered since the world ended, he says.

—Fuckin' Air Supply survives the apocalypse, Meleah says.

—Just think, Nancy says to Michael, that was gonna be y'all's song.

Meleah begins laughing so hard that soon they all are.

They laugh for a long, long while, and maybe even cry some, but eventually they return to the silence that seems to be the truest soundtrack for the state of the world and their plight in it.

This section of Highway 73 is also littered with random debris and abandoned vehicles.

A baby stroller. A tandem bicycle. A gun safe. An oven. Three huge wooden crosses.

An older model station wagon is slanted across the road with all its doors open. A small four-wheel drive Toyota truck lies on its side, its windshield missing.

He slowly drives around each object in the road, often pulling onto the frozen shoulder and occasionally into the ditch.

It's slow going, but they're warm and have no interest in going anywhere fast.

With each little driveway they pass, a palpable tension enters the warm cab and Nancy grips the knife in her hand even harder.

To their left, TriState Off Road Park, a popular place for bog-ins and races, has been leveled and is littered with vehicles and the dead.

Hundreds of corpses frozen in place, the cold slowing down decay.

An overturned backhoe and a large electrical truck with a lift are covered in dead bodies.

So are the stands.

And the vehicles scattered about, overturned and not, are filled with the dead.

The girls don't see it. Meleah's eyes are closed and Nancy's looking out the passenger window at the woods on the opposite side, and he doesn't call attention to it, just drives on.

A few miles more and a small wooden house with a couple of semi-trucks parked in its yard has a piece of plywood with a message spray painted on it that he can't quite make out and doesn't stop to read.

They need to find a place to stop, to rest, to sleep, to eat, to heal, but given how traumatized they are, he can't imagine either girl will be hip to the idea—especially Nancy.

As they approach the caution light at the intersection of County Road 392, he eases off the gas and slows.

Nancy sits up, wary. In between them, Meleah opens her eyes.

—You're not stopping, Nancy says.

—Looking for a place to.

—But—

—I know, but we need to. We need to eat and sleep and hydrate.

—*Sleep*? I'll never sleep again.

—I'm so sorry for what happened last night, he says. I won't let that happen again.

—How're you gonna—

—I'll go in alone, sweep the place. You two will stay outside, weapons out and ready. If a place is clear and we're reasonably certain it's safe, we'll take turns keeping watch. We'll be ready at all times. All of us.

Meleah nods. Nancy seems to think about it.

Beneath the caution light, which no longer blinks, sits the remnants of a head-on collision—a Chevy Silverado extended-cab truck and a huge old Buick, their grills and front quarter panels crumpled, drivers' doors opened.

Ahead on the left is the home of a man he knew a long time ago.

At one point, a while back—maybe ten years or more—Michael started a community theater in Wewa called the Tupelo. In it, he taught classes, conducted workshops, and produced plays he had penned. It was located in the appliance and furniture side of his dad's old hardware store building. Most everything in the small theater space was donated—including the seating, a set of old wooden church pews that the man who lived in the house next to him now had helped obtain from a local small country church.— We'll have a wall behind us so we'll be facing anyone coming at us, he says, and we'll have an escape route planned out.

—I don't know, Nancy says. I wasn't really planning on going into any other houses.

—Ever?

She shrugs.

—Maybe I could keep watch from outside, she says.

—It's up to you, he says. But I promise you, I won't let anyone get the drop on us like that ever again.

She doesn't respond.

—I understand if you don't believe me.

—We'll see.

—Okay. I'm gonna check the house there on the left.

—What? Now?

—Good people lived there before all this happened.

10

Hedges lining a chain link fence.

Trees in the yard.

Bushes. Shrubs. Saplings.

Tin barn in the back.

—The fence is undisturbed, Michael says. The house looks good.

—Nothing looked particularly wrong with the one last night, Nancy says.

—Should've never gone that far off the road. Won't make that mistake again.

Driving around the wreck, he turns left on 392 and pulls up to the front gate.

Jumping out, he grabs his gear from the back and gets back in the warm cab.

Reaching into one of the duffels, he withdraws two knives, gives one to Meleah and places the other in his pocket. He then gives each of the girls a revolver.

—Please be careful. Keep it pointed down and away

from us. Don't put your finger on the trigger until you're ready to use it. When you have to use it, point at the biggest part of the target—the chest or midsection—or whatever is closest. Hold it steady with both hands and gently squeeze the trigger. Don't pull it. And try not to move the gun when you shoot. The first chamber in both of them is empty for safety. So when you really need to shoot something or someone, the first click will be a dry fire. Squeeze the trigger again right away. Okay?

—Okay, Meleah says.

Nancy nods.

—I'm gonna leave y'all here with the truck running. Meleah, stay behind the wheel. Both of you, have your weapons ready. If something happens, just drive away.

—I can't—

—Don't hesitate, he says. Just drive. Please. For me.

She nods.

—Keep an eye out while I'm inside. Watch behind you. To the sides. Around the house. If I run out, don't shoot me. If it's not me, shoot.

They both nod.

—There are plenty of provisions in my bags. Weapons. Gas masks. There's plenty of gas in the cans. Drive as far as you can on the truck, then switch to the ATV. Try to make it to Wewa. Nearly anyone left there—if there's anyone left—will help you.

—Just come back, Meleah says. Fast. Don't make us wait long.

—You got it.

He lifts the 9mm from the seat between his legs and clips it to his waistband. He then removes the short shotgun from the bag and gets out.

Meleah slides over behind the wheel and he leans in and hugs her.

—I love you, he says.

—Love you, she says. See you in just a few minutes.

He reaches over to Nancy.

She reluctantly extends her hand.

He takes it and squeezes it.

—Thank you for everything. You're a resilient young woman. Don't let the monsters win. Process their poison out of your system so you don't become like them.

—How do I do that?

—Meleah can tell you. Good conversation for y'all to have while I'm gone.

He stands upright again.

—Lock your doors and wish me luck.

—Praying for you, Meleah says.

He locks and closes the door and turns and walks toward the house.

As he nears the house, he smells it.

Death.

The unmistakable stench of decay hits him when he's still several feet from the house, and he turns around and walks back to the truck.

—What is it? Meleah asks as she opens the door.

—Just need to find another place, he says.

She nods and slides over.

He climbs back in, placing the shotgun facedown on the floorboard between them, turns the truck around, navigates around the wreck at the intersection, and continues south on Highway 73.

He passes a few other houses on either side of the road before reaching a trailer up on the right with a wooden hand-painted sign out front that reads: Pat's Hair Fashions.

—How about there? he asks, pointing to a tin shed on the far edge of the property.

Enclosed on all sides but the front, the shed looks more like a garage or even a small house than a shed.

—I like how open it is, Meleah says, but it won't provide much warmth.

—We could back the truck into it, he says. Get blankets from some of the houses around here. Two sleep in the back while one sits in the cab on watch. If anybody comes up, whoever's on post wakes us and drives off.

—Look back there, Nancy says.

Behind the Pat's Hair Fashions trailer there's another trailer—two more on opposite sides of the field beyond it.

—That's a lot of places to have to check, she says.

—True, he says. We're getting close to—

A knock at the window causes them all to jump.

Coming up with his 9mm he sees an elderly woman with dirty gray hair and a waxen, heavily wrinkled face.

She holds her hands up.

—Don't shoot. I'm here to help.

They all begin to search the area around them as he rolls down the window.

—You need to get out of here or at least get your truck off the road as fast as you can, she says. Turn around and go back wherever you came from, or you can hide it behind my place. But just for tonight.

He doesn't say anything, just continues to look around.

—It's just me, she says. I'm alone as a body can be. I'm willin' to help y'all but I ain't getting kilt over it. What's it gonna be? Turn around and head back. Follow me to my place. Stay here and get kilt.

—Where do you live? Michael asks. Where is your place?

—Back corner of the field, she says, pointing to the trailer in the back right. Ain't got much food. Nothin' worth stealin'. But you can get some rest and sleep tonight if you like.

He thinks about it.

—Well, I'm heading back there now. Either follow me or have a good if short life. If you do come back, follow the drive 'til the very back, then cut across the field so your tracks can't be seen from up here.

She then walks to the back of the truck and disappears from view for a moment. In another moment, she comes out pedaling a once burgundy, now mostly rusty old trike, a Schwinn Meridian, with baskets in front and back full of plastic grocery bags.

She pedals far faster than seems possible, scooting

down the drive leading to the trailer on the left.

—An old woman on a fuckin' tricycle was able to sneak up on us? Nancy says.

—Embarrassing, Michael says.

—What do y'all think? Meleah says. Should we stay with her tonight?

—Could be a trap, Nancy says. They send her out to lure unsuspecting idiots in for dinner—or worse.

—We could do what we were going to do before. Y'all can stay in the truck, weapons up, while I go in and check out the place. Could search the other trailers too and the woods.

—I think we could stay, Meleah says. Not sure how much farther we can go. We really need to stop and eat and rest. Everything we do is a risk. This one seems better than most. I don't think she was lying and I take her warning to get off the road seriously.

11

—**Y**'all been through enough to earn your paranoia? the old lady asks.

They've just finished their search of the other trailers on the property and are inside her small trailer with her.

—And then some, Michael says.

—Sorry to hear that, she says. I truly am.

The narrow living room of the single-wide mobile home is dim and musty, its cheap furniture and those sitting on it seen in the wave of candlelight.

—I'm Michael, by the way, he says. This is Meleah and that's Nancy.

—Nice to make your acquaintance, she says. I'm Vera. My son's name is Vern.

Her son, a large, soft, fleshy boy who is actually her grandson, is asleep on the couch.

—And I'll warn you before he wakes up, she says. Vern ain't right in the head.

—Whatta you mean? Nancy asks.

—He's a good, sweet boy, but he's dim. Brain doesn't

work quite right. He's fifteen and acts five.

—We have weapons, Nancy says. We're strangers. The world is a dark, bad place. Why would you invite us into your home?

—If I told you, you'd think I was a few sandwiches short of a picnic.

—You've got us intrigued now, Meleah says.

Vera smiles.

She's not as old as he first thought. If it's-not-the-age-but-the-milage was true before the end of the world, it's doubly true now.

—God speaks to me. I knew y'all were all right before I ever tapped on your window. Call me crazy if you like, but ask yourself how me and my boy have survived this long?

They nod, but don't say anything.

Vera looks directly at Michael, their eyes locking.

—You're a kind, gentle man. Very loving. So's your daughter. And she has great wisdom—far beyond her years. And this poor thing . . .

She looks at Nancy.

—. . . is wounded, but has much goodness in her. Y'all would no more intentionally harm me and my boy as each other.

He hadn't told her Meleah was his daughter. They hadn't told her anything but their names.

—Whatta you think? she says.

—That there are more things in heaven and earth, Horatio, than are dreamt of in your philosophy, he says.

—What's that—

—We don't think you're crazy, Meleah says.

—She does, Vera says, nodding toward Nancy.

—Actually, I do, but I like crazies. They're my tribe.

—Mama? Vern says waking, drowsy and disoriented. Mama. Mama, who are these people?

—Just some of Mama's friends.

—I thought we didn't have many friends now and no new ones.

—That's right, she says. You're right. But these are some of Mama's old friends. They just came for a short visit.

—I'm hungry, he says.

—Me too, she says. And so are our guests. Let's eat.

Michael begins digging into the duffel at his feet, but she stops him.

—Y'all are our guests tonight, she says. You'll share in our portion. Come on. Everyone to the table.

They make their way over to the dining table, Meleah and Nancy sharing at seat.

Vera begins to open cans of vegetables and place them on the table.

—Open a few more of these while I get some plates.

Michael takes the can opener and proceeds to open a can of ravioli and another of clam chowder, both of which remind him of Dawn.

—We're using plates, Mama? Vern says.

—It's a special night, Vera says.

She places mismatched plastic plates before them and hands out forks. She then sticks spoons in the cans.

—Meleah, will you light some more of those candles? It'll be dark soon. I'll pour us some water.

—Can I have juice, Mama?

—We're out of juice. Be a good boy and drink water for Mama, okay?

—Okay, Mama. I will.

She places paper cups on the table in front of them and carefully pours water from a gallon jug into them.

—Help yourselves, she says when she finishes. When everyone has fixed their plates I'll say grace.

Vern reaches for a can across the table from him and knocks another one over.

—Let Mama do yours, okay?

—Okay.

When the plates are full, she bows her head and everyone follows her lead.

—For what we're about to receive, make us truly

thankful. And bless our special guests.

Everyone begins to eat.

—This is really good, Michael says. It's so kind of you to share with us.

—Be not forgetful to entertain strangers, she says. For thereby some have entertained angels unawares.

He smiles.

—Hebrews, he says, then nodding toward Meleah and Nancy adds, And I have no doubt those two are angels. And so are you and your son for us tonight. Thank you.

—Is Hebrews as close as you can get? she asks.

—Afraid so, he says. I'm actually surprised I remembered that.

—Chapter thirteen verse two.

—Never would've gotten that, he says.

They eat in silence for a while, the only sound that of fork tines coming into contact with plastic plates and occasionally teeth.

—The Kinard Library carried some of your books, Vera says. Read a lot of them.

—Really? Thank you.

—He's always been big in Kinard, Meleah says.

Nancy laughs.

—Obscure most everywhere else, he adds, but huge in Kinard.

—Liked the ones with the prison chaplain detective the best, Vera says.

—Thank you, he says. Those were my firsts and favorites too.

—Got a pretty good imagination, don't you? You ever imagine anything like this?

—No ma'am, I didn't. Nothing remotely like this.

12

First watch.

Everyone asleep except Michael.

Hiss of a gas heater. Flicker of candlelight. Dim, drowsy night.

Outside a cold wind blows, whistling through the pines, rattling the trailer, clanging a loose piece of tin, quieting the howls, shrieks, and screeches coming from the woods.

He's in an uncomfortable upright chair by a window in the living room. Meleah and Nancy are asleep on the pullout sofa bed across from him.

Somehow Meleah is sleeping hard. Beside her, Nancy's fitful attempt at sleep is accompanied by unintelligible mumblings full of both anger and sadness.

From down the narrow hallway, Vera eases into the room.

—How's it going? she asks.

He nods and shrugs.

She sits in a chair across from him.

—Pretty quiet, actually, he says. Are they always like this here?

—The Angries? The bitterer the cold, the better it is. Wind helps.

—Angries? he says.

—Angries. Crazies. Ragers. Nighters. A thing is what it is. Doesn't matter what you call it, now does it?

—And what are those things? he asks.

—Sick. Infected. Rabid. Killers. They're humans with most of the human part turned off.

—They ever come up to the trailer?

—Sometimes. Bang around a bit. Haven't broken in yet.

—You gonna leave before they do?

—And go where? How? On my bike with Vern in the basket? How long you think we'd last out there?

He doesn't respond, just sits with the hopeless reality of her situation.

—What about you? she says. Where will you go back to?

—Not going back, he says. Headed to Wewa.

—You can't. Even if you could, there is no Wewa anymore. Wewa is underwater. Dead Lakes is literal now. That's all it is. One big, watery ghost-town grave yard.

The Dead Lakes, a nearly seven-thousand-acre lake of tannic waters filled with bases of dead bald cypress trees, is—or was when last he saw it—an eerily beautiful body of water. Some two-hundred years ago, the Apalachicola River drifted over and formed a sand bank that created a natural dam for the Chipola River, which then flooded the swamp and killed the millions of bald cypress trees that give it its name.

—But it doesn't matter 'cause you can't get there anyway, she says.

—Because of the flooding? he asks.

—Well, yeah, I guess, but I meant the Rebelz and the Angries.

—I don't follow.

—You can't even get to the flooded area because you can't get through Kinard.

—Why's that?

—The Rebelz. Before all this went down it was a group of boys—young men, whatever—who . . . you know what boys around here are like. They were sort of a redneck hunting club, but more, like best buds that did everything together. Now the ones who're left are like a gang. They run Kinard. Can't get through.

—I've got to.

—It's just two different forms of suicide, she says. By day and the Rebelz get you. By night and the Angries get you. You've got to take these girls and go back.

—I can't. I've got to get to Wewa.

—*There is no Wewa,* she says, frustration at the ragged edges of her voice.

—How many of these Rebelz are there?

—Too many. Don't be a damn fool.

—I've got to get there somehow. Have to figure out a way.

—If you won't listen to a crazy old lady from Kinard, will you listen to someone from Wewa?

—I'm listening to you, but yes, I'd really like to talk to someone from there. Why?

—There's a gal up the road who came out of there.

—Who?

13

—There ain't nothin' left, Chaplain. It's all underwater. All of it. The whole town. You can dive down and see the streets and buildings. It's the freakiest thing I've ever seen.

Erica is a short, squat, fireplug of a coonass country girl, tough as a lighter knot, hardworking as a borrowed mule.

She can hunt and fish and handle herself as well as anyone he's ever known.

She has short black hair, a dark complexion, and dark features.

She was a captain at Gulf Correctional when he was a chaplain there, and they had been good friends ever since. All this time and she still calls him Chaplain.

She has a small fortress not far from where Vera lives. He has come alone. They are in her yard, behind her tall, wooden privacy fence in the early morning.

—Nothing's left? he says, his warm breath showing in the cold air. No one?

—I ain't sayin' there ain't no spots not underwater. Ain't sayin' there ain't a few poor souls left there neither—though how they could be surviving I couldn't say. But the town itself and nearly all, if not all, the people are gone. I'm sorry. I hope your people survived and then got out, but, I'm gonna tell you the truth, Chaplain—not many did. I's at the prison when the first wave came. Walked out right then. Never looked back. Came and got my boat, went and got my girl, headed for the hills. We're gonna go farther eventually, but not sure where to go and we're making it okay for now, so . . .

The girl Erica went and got is Lindsay, a tall, thin, aloof blonde with an angular face, pale skin, and light blue eyes.

Lindsay had just walked out and handed them each a cup of coffee.

—Have you been back? he asks.

—Went back a time or two, just looking, she says, her breath even more visible after sipping the coffee. Didn't see much. Didn't make it too far neither though. I's mostly curious about the town. Heard about those places where the entire city is underwater. Wanted to see for myself.

He nods and thinks about it.

The yard is mostly sandy dirt with a few small trees and shrubs and a gazebo. It fronts a doublewide mobile home and is surrounded by a wooden slat fence some eight feet tall.

—You're goin' no matter what I say, ain't ya? Erica says.

He nods.

—Got to, he says. If there's even the remotest possibility that anybody survived.

She nods.

—I get it. It was me, I'd do the same. First thing I did was go get her.

She nods toward Lindsay.

Lindsay lifts her coffee mug in a *cheers* gesture, but the expression on her implacable face doesn't change.

—How are things here? he asks, looking around at their setup.

—Good, she says. Really good. No one bothers us. Location is great and the fence really helps.

—The people in the woods—the altered or infected or whatever they are—they don't give you any trouble?

She shakes her head.

—Don't seem to be as many here, she says. They don't climb, so the fence keeps 'em out. Keep thinkin' they'll starve or get better or move on to somewhere else. I don't know.

—Were there any in Wewa? he asks.

She nods.

—But climbing ain't the only thing they don't do. They don't swim. Seem to avoid the water like they do the day.

He thinks about it and they both sip on their coffee.

He's never been a coffee drinker. Iced tea was his caffeinater before the end. But this warm, strong, sweet substance is as good as anything he's had in two months.

—What's the story with the Rebelz? he asks.

—Fistful of assholes, she says. Good ol' boy meth heads. One of 'em's my cousin. Another I helped out of a jam when he was inside. They don't mess with us.

He thinks about it. She studies him as he does.

—What're you gettin' at? she says, her eyes lighting up, amusement on her face.

—Could my daughter and the girl who saved us stay with you while I make a run into Wewa?

—Chaplain, not only can they stay, and we'll protect them as if they were our own, but you can borrow my boat and scuba gear.

14

Meleah shakes her head.

—I don't like the idea of you going alone.

They are standing out behind Vera's trailer. Michael is checking his gear and getting ready to unload the ATV.

—It's just a little boat ride, he says. I'll be back before dark. You'll be far safer here.

—What about you? she says.

He doesn't want to leave her, doesn't want her out of his sight, but wants her as safe and secure as she can possibly be in this new reality.

—Plus, he says, with more room in the boat I'll be able to bring more people back. I'll check Taylor and his parents' place. If he's there, I'll have him here by dinner.

—Check the church, she says. They would've turned it into a shelter.

He nods.

—You really trust Erica this much? she asks.

He nods again.

—Given the state of the world, I can't think of a

safer, better place for you. Anywhere.

—With you, she says.

Is he making a mistake? Should he take her? He's just not certain. He wants to take her—part of him insists on it, but he really does believe she'll be safer here.

—It's safer with her until I get back, he says.

—Okay. If you really think it's the thing to do.

The back door opens and Nancy walks out, pulling her coat up around her.

He tells her the plan.

—No way, she says.

—But—

—I've saved your ass twice already, she says. Who's gonna do it if I'm not there?

—That's why I want you here, he says, looking after everyone. Help keep them safe. If we all go, there's no room for anyone else on the boat.

—Not all, just me, she says. I'm little. Don't take up much room.

—I'd worry about Meleah the entire time we were gone. But with you here to help keep an eye on—

—You'll worry about her anyway.

—I'll worry about you too, he says. But less if y'all are back here with Erica. Please.

—Okay, she says, but I ain't bein' anybody's lesbian lover.

15

Alone. Again.

Lonely. Again.

He's in a fourteen-foot fiberglass bateau with a 30-horsepower Johnson motor on it gliding across brackish water where Highway 71 should be—and he guesses still is some thirty feet below.

Erica had driven him to the Dead Lakes' new water's edge near the intersection of Highway 73 and 71where her boat had been hidden, helped him load the craft with gas and gear, and returned to help protect Meleah and Nancy.

Now it is just him, alone in this new watery world.

The tall tops of pine trees on either side of him peek out only a few feet above the water, having the odd appearance of a type of pine shrub that doesn't exist—or didn't in the previous iteration of the world.

It is much warmer here. And less gray. In a few spots there are even holes in the low charcoal clouds that hint at blue sky beyond.

Leaving Meleah, after losing her and finding her and

nearly losing her again, was one of the most difficult things he's ever had to do, and he's still unsure it was the right thing to do.

Was it a mistake?

Part of him wants to turn the boat around right now, to go back and get her, to bring her along with him, but if he did and something happened to her . . .

But what if something happens because you left her?

Will he see her again?

Will he ever see anyone again?

Is Dawn waiting for him up ahead in the small flooded town that would forever be home? Is Micah? Is anyone?

Will he make it back? Will Meleah be there waiting for him if he does?

Doesn't seem like it, not in this moment when he feels like the last and only person on the planet.

Up ahead he sees the massive floating fuselage of a commercial airplane. The bright blue lets him know it belonged to Southwest.

Now it belongs to no one. Like everything else in the world it simply is—abandoned, forsaken, or in some cases being used by someone other than the original owner.

The enormous downed plane fills him with dread and he wants to turn back, wants to figure out a better way to do this, find some help, hedge his bets against a world where there are no longer any planes in the sky and some are floating in the flooded outskirts of his small town, which in the entirety of its history has never even had an airport.

As he nears and navigates around what's left of the immense aircraft, he can see through the small windows and open doors the rotting corpses of passengers still buckled to their seats, the yellow oxygen cups still strapped to their skulls, the plastic bags and tubing floating up around them.

He swallows hard and gives the plane an even wider berth.

Turn around or continue forward?

Something bumps his boat.

He slows and looks down.

It's a dead body floating in the water.

When he hits another, he looks around to see that he's surrounded by them. An entire field of facedown floating bodies.

He cuts the engine and drifts among the dead.

He'd seen something similar in a small town in Georgia on his way back home, but they had been on dry land, littering the streets and sidewalks and parking lots of what once had been places where people congregated.

This is far more disturbing, far more eerie in its unexpectedness and unnaturalness.

There's nothing to indicate the bodies have any connection to the plane, and he doesn't think they do—something that makes it even more frightening and disquieting.

If you're looking for signs . . . a downed plane and a field of dead bodies are pretty big ones.

Not looking for signs. Looking for Dawn and Micah, for my family and friends.

Passing what he believes is the last of the dead bodies, he pulls the crank to start the motor.

It sputters to life.

He continues.